Chasing Palms

Books by Jonathan Herbert

Butch Sands Series
Banyan Street
Silver King
Chasing Palms

Coming Soon!
Butch Sands Series
Leeward Run

Chasing Palms

Jonathan Herbert

SPEAKING VOLUMES, LLC
NAPLES, FLORIDA
2024

Chasing Palms

Copyright © 2016 by Jonathan Herbert

All rights reserved. No part of this book may be reproduced or transmitted in any form or by any means without written permission.

ISBN 979-8-89022-163-6

For Roy King

Acknowledgments

I am truly grateful for the loving support from my wife, Angela, and our two children.

The completion of this novel was possible because of invaluable contributions made by Michael Kinney and James Biery.

The best way out is always through.
—Robert Frost

Chapter One

Chase Anderson stood in the second level foyer of his abandoned stilt house and watched the incoming tide run along a mangrove coastline that wrapped itself around sugar sand and bent palms. His sharp pale features and streaked blonde hair absorbed the last rays of sunlight as he gripped a worn baseball the way he would a two-seam fastball. Blood stains covered his right shoulder and he struggled to breathe.

"Feel that Butch?" Chase asked. "Feel that sunlight?"

"Yeah, I feel it," I said.

"Part of me dies when I watch a sunset. Grace always made me watch them on days I wasn't working late. She said her day wasn't complete without one. It took losing her to finally know what she meant."

"You need a hospital. You've lost too much blood."

He nodded and looked through the oversized squares where pane glass windows should be. This place seemed to speak to his loneliness and despair, like an addiction, his sullen face showed a need for saltwater and warmth.

"Every three days or so, I drive up from North Miami to watch it," Chase said. "Anytime I need a drink . . . when police work fails to give my life purpose . . . you don't get this on the East Coast."

The house faced Gasparilla Sound, a sacred body of water from my youth. The very place my older brother, Kevin taught me how to long drift for Tarpon. I stood in the middle of the room without responding and watched the distant blue waterline with my own thoughts about Kevin and where he might be now. I can only hope he's not dead. Our shared vision of Tatum Jones and his final moments alive put an end to several maddening days of violence across Florida.

"We did an important thing. I know you're worried about your brother right now but believe me, he's never felt better. Justice, be damned."

There is a cracked seawall twenty feet below that protects the narrow wooden legs of the house. Faded blue paint outlines the untreated wood panels below a hurricane damaged metal roof and a line of mature coconut palms parallel to a plot of sand and gravel where the concrete driveway was supposed to have been poured. Pedro Island is a distant barrier against the ever-changing currents that move in from the Gulf of Mexico.

Chase Anderson was once named Mr. Baseball in the state of Florida. The award itself meant something to him, but where he ended up after baseball diminished it. He never favored pitching, but it was the only commonality he ever shared with his self-absorbed father.

Irony made its way inside the creases of his roller coaster life. The same day he was cut by a third minor league team, he received a call from the Miami Police department. His young auspicious wife of two years was found dead from an apparent heroin overdose. Her body covered by a Florida Marlins beach towel, motionless between two large sabal palms near a high-rise hotel. A night out with girlfriends turned violent after she agreed to try something she had never tried before. And now, whenever he drives by a baseball diamond, something inside wakes up and the disappointment of losing her and baseball in the same moment shows in his irascible expression. No way would he lose their house, too.

His decision to quit pitching went mostly unnoticed by major league baseball scouts and he spent the next few years pursuing the only thing that fed his sanity, catching every possible heroin dealer in Greater Miami. His prize target was Tatum Jones, the last person to call his wife's cell phone. Every lead, every undercover bust gives him hope to find this illusive killer known on Miami streets as Tone.

I first met Chase Anderson inside a cramped room with two facing brown chairs and a round table with gang signs etched in the oak legs. He came at me with a full charge of energy. The temperamental detective repeated questions over and over and smoked hand rolled cigarettes. His flush red cheeks moved side to side, and he talked with lanky arms that dropped to emphasize each point of contention. He used strange metaphors when my answers frustrated him, "Butch . . . you're just a proud lion with no appetite. No reason in the world to hide a million dollars on some remote island, right? Where's Cayo Costa Island? East or West coast?"

"I'm not talking without an attorney," I said.

My police report was scattered across the table. The less I talked, the more he paced. He finally stopped to look at the report, twenty minutes after I sat down. "Butch Sands, a lone survivor even? This is made for television. Small town reporter escapes death with millions."

Before I continue on about Chase Anderson and his contempt for being assigned to my case, I should mention Hailey Thomas and our recent engagement that has given me a false sense of security. I should be flying home from a weeklong vacation with her, preparing to go back to work reporting on the quiet streets of Pedro Island. There are necessary things about our rustic boring life that I have not had in weeks. These often help me forget about the corrupt cities and back roads of South Florida.

Less than a month ago, I was left to die on a desolate island. But without detailing everything that happened to me, the truth is, I just want the life outside my corner office window inside the *Island Courier* news building. The palm trees that bend over clear blue inlets where tarpon shadows fold inside thick mangroves and banyan trees that line side roads ending with coarse Bermuda plots of beachfront property, the humid morning streets and seafood trucks unloading before sunrise. Hailey Thomas smiling with brown eyes, folded arms over a white tablecloth, and a burning candle. The smell of coconut shrimp and pan seared red snapper. The clank of pint glasses at the bar and buzz of tourists talking over locals tucked beneath cigar smoke on chairs in the dark corners of Marker 17 Tavern, a centerpiece of Pedro Island.

Weekly stresses from unrealistic deadlines enforced by my overanxious editor about news that means nothing outside this small island community. News that matters to me the same way it matters to Hailey. We built this island life together and hope to hold on as long as possible.

The one person lost in this is Kevin, my noble brother, who insisted on driving me to Miami for that scheduled meeting with Chase Anderson. Kevin and I share an understanding about most things. We truly trust one another the way brothers should, but our lives will never be the same after what happened on this road trip, and the aftermath.

Kevin left Pedro Island late last night saying it wasn't safe to know him anymore. He said killing her murderer was unavoidable and that he lost all desire for living when his first and only love was murdered. He insisted that Hailey and I could still chase our dream.

* * *

It happened about a week ago, on a Thursday morning in the inclement heat of the Everglades. I stood pumping gas beneath a rustic canopy. Traffic moved with urgency beyond the worn asphalt. Wind swept lives passed green swampland and disappeared inside the calescent black line of Alligator Alley.

Kevin and his unsuspecting crush, Rose, were inside the convenience store. We had been driving Eastbound across Florida for over an hour and needed fuel. I felt the stubble on my chin and thought about the meeting I had in two hours with Miami Police. They had been calling for weeks, leaving the same message, "Butch, this is Chase Anderson with Miami PD. I've made several attempts to reach you. No need to explain, you know why I left my number the first time. Call me back."

A call was finally made at the request of my editor, Dudas, and concerned fiancée, Hailey. They know most of the truth about what happened to me in a Key West bar almost a month ago, followed by my time marooned on a no name island. They know nothing about the buried money I'm protecting for someone.

I have not slept well in weeks. Nights run together like one of twenty unsolved crossword puzzles scattered in my top desk drawer. Television makes it worse, so I walk the quiet streets of Pedro Island and try to forget things that happened to me. Truth and evidence live in the depths of my subconscious, far beyond the Florida Keys. I have seen the sunrise three straight days from the seawall at the end of Banyan Street and find clarity each morning when the last rays of light ascend over the distant blue waterline. This is the moment my story comes to life. And once the new day starts, I am reminded of this meeting with Chase Anderson and know it will be a grind.

Luck saved me on that island. A stranger helped me live at the cost of fulfilling a promise. So, I did. And now, to start new with Hailey, I had to clear my name.

The fuel pump clicked off just as a watermelon truck came to a stop near a boiled peanuts stand. Workers jumped from the bed of the truck and immediately began moving watermelons to the storefront. A black Rolls Royce pulled in next. The driver stepped out. Smoke from a cigar rose over his dark face and puffy Afro. I noticed his white gloves as he reached for the fuel pump.

Kevin held Rose's hand as they walked out of the store and around the workers. Both seemed to notice the mint condition of the car. The rear window came down and Kevin removed his blue tinted sunglasses and rubbed his bushy beard. He made eye contact with the driver.

"Can I help you with something?" the driver asked.

"No," Kevin said. "Never mind, I just—"

The driver's gaze wandered away from Kevin to something overhead. I turned to look in the same direction and spotted a seaplane. It approached the busy road, half a mile from the East, and landed into oncoming traffic.

"Oh my God!" Rose screamed.

The seaplane accelerated in front of a moving station wagon, cut off a semi-truck, and turned across the median directly toward us. I was amazed the wings stayed level with the hard turn.

"Boss!" the driver said with panic in his voice. "What is it?" the man asked from the rear window. "I think Tone followed us."

The driver climbed back inside and started the engine. A loud buzzing sound came from the propellers as the seaplane taxied. Watermelons were dropped on the pavement and the entire crew of workers scattered.

A shirtless man with tattoo-covered arms bolted from the cockpit. He ran and jumped on the black hood with a tec-9 in hand. The Rolls Royce came to a screeching stop.

"Out of the car!" the man said.

I noticed a second man step down from the cockpit without much urgency. He was dark skinned, wore a black double-breasted suit, and held two .44 magnums. Tattoos covered the side of his neck and face, one teardrop just under his right eye, a small cross of gold hung around his neck. He fired one round in the air and smiled at the chaotic scene.

"You can't run forever," he said. "Your time is up, old friend."

I looked over at Kevin. He leaned in to bear hug Rose's petite frame. Both gave their full attention to the gunmen.

"Tone!" the man inside the Rolls Royce said.

"Vamanos!"

"Muy bueno."

His shirtless comrade jumped off the hood and walked over to join him. A long pause came next, everyone watched with anticipation. A nod preceded a shower of bullets and the deafening sounds of combustion and steel-on-steel power. Tires spun in reverse, and I fell to the ground to crawl under the truck. A sudden sting shot through my left leg as sparks danced around tires and growing puddles of gasoline.

The gunfire finally stopped, and all sounds were muted. I watched both men run across the parking lot. Flip-flops stepped up and out of sight inside the seaplane. My leg burned from the bullet graze. I rolled over to see the target. The driver hung from a partially opened door full of gray holes. Blood spilled down his arm, staining the white gloves. There was no movement from the rear door, also full of bullet holes.

Horns sounded from the road. I used the truck door to stand as the seaplane taxied through traffic. The camera in the backseat caught my attention. I grabbed it just as the seaplane turned around in the grassy median and passed the gas station for takeoff. I focused the lens and took two shots just before its ascent.

I sat down on the filthy asphalt and held my pulsating leg with the smell of smoke and burning steel everywhere. I looked over at the front entrance and saw Kevin pushing down on Rose's chest. Blood covered her shirt. She was unconscious.

* * *

I hoped Rose would live. A constant rush of adrenaline moved through me, even now, twenty hours after that bullet grazed my leg. Gunfire and panic slammed together inside two minutes of terror. Those menacing eyes and tattoo covered arms burned in my short-term. I could still hear the screaming targets, smell the gasoline, and see the crimson blood splattered across my brother's beard and sunglasses.

I looked at my unfamiliar reflection in the mirror windows of a Miami Hospital. My torn khaki shorts and blood-stained shirt smelled of benzene. I felt the coarse Bermuda grass under bare feet.

In the hours waiting, I watched palm trees draw long shadows across the asphalt parking lot. The emergency doors would constantly open and close. I watched them with anticipation and wondered how Kevin would react to fatal news. Rose was his first love. Only I knew this because he told me he loved her. Rose had no idea.

Kevin finally appeared. His hands clutched white running shoes. His sunglasses hung from a wire and tears collected in bloodshot eyes. The moment floored me, and I knew before he said anything. His sullen face said everything as he found a seat on a bench.

"Smoke?" Kevin asked.

"I don't have any. What did the doc say?"

Kevin leaned forward and looked at the white shoes. His head dropped. He cleared his throat and raised dark eyebrows the way our late father always would before he said something important.

"Rose bought these last week . . . thought I'd start running with her. She said white makes you look faster than you are. She was always doing things for me. I told her I wanted to start running. That was her, always thinking of others first."

"Sorry, Kev."

"Should've told her how I felt. I loved her. Never felt that before her. She was the one, Butch. I almost had it."

"What's that?"

"The life."

I looked past my reeling brother at a waiting, unmarked police cruiser. The driver made a hand gesture at me. I wanted to stay with Kevin but knew it was time to go.

"They're waiting, Kev. I can't believe this happened to her. I'm so sorry."

"Get it over with, Butch. We came down here to clear your name in the first place. I should go inside. Doc is probably waiting."

I stood and shared silence with my defeated brother. We hugged for the first time in years, then turned and walked away in opposite directions. Once inside the unmarked cruiser, I sat back in the big cloth seat without saying a word and turned to watch Kevin enter the hospital as we drove away toward the Miami skyline.

Chapter Two

A lone ceiling fan cut through the stench of stale coffee. I wanted this meeting to end soon and felt ready yesterday. But today, I cannot think clearly about any of the reasons that brought me here.

There was a sudden change in Chase Anderson when Chief Diggs walked in the room and sat down across from me. The broad-shouldered man scanned my police report with oval bifocals. He finished reading the first page and sat back in his chair. Both hands rubbed a cleanly shaven brown head as he took in a deep breath followed by a long exhale. Chase reacted to him the way a neglected child would do something for attention.

"I've got this one," Chase said. "Let me handle the questioning this time."

"Too much money involved, Anderson," Chief Diggs said. "This needs to be sent down to the district attorney's office."

Both men stared at me for what felt like a full minute. I cleared my throat and shifted in the uncomfortable wooden chair.

"At least we know Butch Sands exists," Chief Diggs said. "May as well have been a ghost."

"We only need a few minutes to sign off on this, right?" Chase asked. "He just tells us where he's hiding the rest of the money and we'll agree to a plea bargain. No lawyers?"

I looked up and made direct eye contact with Chase and reminded myself to say as little as possible without a lawyer present. Chase flicked ash on the floor and held his arms up the way a referee signals for a made field goal.

"I'm not talking without a lawyer," I said.

"First you hit a Key West cop, and then you skip a court hearing. What leverage do you have, even with a lawyer?"

I stayed silent and countered direct eye contact from Chase. His cheeks were red, but the initial nervousness was gone with his boss in the room. He pulled a soft pack of cigarettes from his white shirt pocket and began to pack it against the bottom of his hand.

"This one should be cake, Chief Diggs. Frat boys are easier to break than most of the scumbags I deal with downtown."

Chief Diggs turned toward me and nodded approval. He probably assumed I was a college student, maybe a below average business major at some Florida community college.

"What college, Butch?" Chief Diggs asked.

"No college," I said.

Chase laughed and moved in closer to my chair. I could smell the cigarette smoke on his clothes.

"Unshaven, hair's a mess. You wear this shirt all week, Butch? If not college then what? You obviously don't have a job the way you present yourself. You're a mess."

The chief joined in with a low bellowing laugh. Chase pushed away from my chair and stood upright. He lit another cigarette. A long pause followed the laughter. They waited for my reaction, but I was in no mood for laughing. My mind was on Kevin, still out there, alone inside a strange hospital with a dead girlfriend.

Chief Diggs reached for his vibrating cell phone. Putting it to his ear, he closed his eyes. Chase turned his attention away from me.

"Tatum Jones? Was it him?" Chase asked.

"Remember this morning?"

"You're off that case, Anderson," Chief Diggs said.

Chase stepped aside as the chief stood up from the table. Both men looked at me then at each other. I thought about offering to leave them alone but decided to stay put.

"We can't discuss this right now, Anderson," Chief Diggs said. "You've had more chances than most seasoned guys get for a case like that."

"But I'm close—"

"Forget Jones. Focus on this case for now. And remember, half the money is still missing. Butch may be your only chance at finding it."

"Excuse me, Butch," the Chief said. "Something urgent has come up."

"I understand."

Chase waited for Chief Diggs to leave before he sat down across from me. He looked at the scattered pages between us. My name in bold letters. My actions italicized. Life altering experiences broken down to a ten-digit case number.

The dollar amount listed as missing caught my attention. There was more than a hundred thousand dollars buried on Cayo Costa Island. Chase took a drag from the cigarette and adjusted his collar.

"I know a lot about you," Chase said. "So, let's make this quick. I should be leaving with Chief Diggs but am stuck with you."

"We can reschedule."

"No way, you're as hard to pin down as one of my undercover heroin dealers. Something broke in a case I've been tracking for almost two years now. Big time trafficker gunned down a Miami Politician at a gas station of all places. From a seaplane of all things."

I knew he had no idea about my connection to the same shooting. He put the cigarette out under the table and smirked. His focus was on everything but me. I took this opportunity to end this pointless meeting.

"I need to get back to the hospital."

"What? We're just getting started here."

I stood from the table and headed for the door again. My leg hurt with every step. The bullet had grazed my left calf and an unexpected pain shot through my leg with each step.

"Sit your ass down, Sands."

I stepped away from his wide blue eyes and flush red face. His attention was back on me. The doorknob jiggled and he grabbed it.

"All good Francine," Chase said. "Everything is under control in here."

I turned from the door and grabbed the stack of paperwork on the table. Before he could react, I tossed it in a nearby wastebasket. He leaned over and pulled it out.

"Appears you need me more than I need you," I said. "Sounds like your bosses have some trust issues with one of their rookies."

"Do you know what they do to young white guys in prison?" Chase asked smiling now. "Especially pretty ones."

I sat back down at the table without making eye contact. A stale mate is a hell of a place to be when you are in a hurry. I decided to bring up the shooting.

"Was it the same gas station?" I asked.

"Same? Same as what?"

"Never mind. Let's get back to me and my problems."

"Your case can wait. What do you know about that?"

"Tell me what you know first," I said.

"So, this pilot runs most of the heroin traffic North of Miami to Fort Lauderdale. Never shown his face in public before this morning. He shoots and kills a few people, including one of those hands-across-America; I'm going to protect our children from drugs, politicians. His street name is Tone, but his real name is Tatum Jones. I've been chasing him for a long time. Chief Diggs is meeting with a few witnesses to confirm what we already think."

"So, that's who killed Rose."

"Rose? Who is she?" Chase asked.

I stood up from the table and walked over to the door. Chase followed me out to the hallway.

"Where are you going? Why do you keep limping? We have two hours to get through this. The Atlanta Braves are in town tonight and I have box tickets and a sure thing waiting for me to pick her up."

"Stray bullet grazed my leg during the same gas station shooting. Move, I need to tell Kevin about Tatum."

Chase grabbed my shoulder and hurried by me. We stood face to face in the crowded hallway, both out of breath. I tried to get around him but could sense more people behind me now. There were no outs.

"Eyes right here, Butch. You're surrounded and very close to spending a few nights in county jail. I'm concerned about your leg. Do you need a doctor?"

"I don't think so. Not yet."

"Fine. Now, personally, I think you're hiding something. But the people around you, your editor, fiancée, and brother all vouch for you. Can you believe that?"

"Why wouldn't they? I was kidnapped and should've died on that island."

"We'll get to your case in a minute. Right now, I need to know why you just reacted like that. Do you know Tatum Jones?"

"I was at the gas station this morning. Tatum killed my brothers' girlfriend, Rose."

"Okay, I understand. Let's first do a little Q and A before we get to Tatum Jones."

"Look, I'm here with good intentions. But what happened yesterday with my brother and his girlfriend. I don't know. She was murdered and I'm standing here with you talking about what? I know what happened. Just tell me how I can cooperate and get this behind me? My brother is alone in a hospital room. Can't this wait?"

"Wait?"

"Yes, wait."

Two street cops forcefully directed me back to the room and made me sit down at the table again. Chase followed us in and lit another cigarette. Smoke rose above neatly combed blonde hair. He picked up the top page with the missing money amount and cleared his throat.

"Tell me if this sounds like something to put off yet another day. Butch Sands. Twenty-two years old, white male. Suspected of double homicide, one count of money laundering, two counts of grand theft, one count of aiding and abetting a known con artist, and finally, my favorite, one count of police evasion."

"I'm innocent."

"Sure, you are. Why not run to us first? If there's nothing to hide, right? Why drive to Gainesville before the Miami Police station? You could've just called the son and told him about his dead father."

I leaned back in the uncomfortable chair and looked up at the ceiling fan. Kevin remained at the forefront of my mind. I wanted to tackle this pompous asshole.

"I fulfilled a promise. He saved my life. Telling his son in person was important."

Chase put both palms on the table. He leaned in close with raised eyebrows.

"Good story, Butch. Now, if I had a dollar for every bullshit sob story about brotherhood and promises that became an excuse for making bonehead decisions, I wouldn't come in tomorrow. I wouldn't need the money they're paying me to catch dealers."

I shrugged and ignored the prodding comments. This was useless without a lawyer. I knew there was nothing left to say that would not be held against me in a court of law. The room temperature was uncomfortably hotter than when we first sat down.

"We know about the con artist. Nobody cares about his death. He was a victim too, just like you. And somehow, you survived . . . and ended up with another man's life savings. What about his three sons and widow? Did they ever cross your mind?"

I had simply followed a dying father's request without thinking about the repercussions on his own life. The missing details in the police report were my own, as was the buried money.

"Am I being charged with a crime?"

"Look, we know there was money. The widow wants to press charges against you if you don't comply. We also know about the money you gave her son. Just tell me where the rest of it is and everything will be dropped. Be a hero, Butch. Not another dealer with something to hide."

There was a long silence as I contemplated a sudden idea. The pictures of the seaplane had to be valuable to Chase Anderson. But could I make him want the pictures?

"I think we can help each other out."

"What are you talking about? How can you help me?" Chase turned stone-faced and backed away from me.

He shook his head and blinked with confusion. Smoke rose between us. I knew he was being pushed to his limit.

"I have pictures of the seaplane."

"Tone's seaplane?" Chase asked.

"Yes."

"Why were you there again? Chief could've mentioned that before you came in. Does he know this?"

"He sent someone to pick me up from the hospital. You didn't know?"

Chase sat back down at the table. He leaned forward, elbows on paper, and stared at the tan walls. I took the opportunity to stand again and open the door. The hallway was empty now.

"We're not done, Butch."

"Are you interested or not?" I asked.

"You know the answer."

Chase was sullen now and spoke in a lower tone. He almost seemed uninterested in the offer. I stayed inside the office and waited for him to make eye contact with me again. I could see defeat in his eyes. The confidence was gone. He was officially out of the Tatum Jones business and there was nothing he could do about it. Chief Diggs had clearly lost trust in him.

"There's a small diner near Naples called Leo's. Be there tomorrow morning around nine. I'll bring Kevin and the pictures of the seaplane."

I turned away before Chase could respond, down the narrow hallway and passed a group of well-dressed lawyers escorting a Latino man in orange prison garb. They moved as one organism without acknowledging me or anyone else. I squeezed by them and limped outside.

Chapter Three

The blood-orange sun hung low over a distant waterline. Brown pelicans glided just above the sand and landed in the strong current that rolled through the wide mouth of the pass. I sat with my back against the glass of the lighthouse and watched the gray strip of beach along neighboring Cayo Costa Island, green and dormant, a few hundred yards away from two tarpon boats.

My aching leg was still loosely wrapped in gauze and medical tape. I kept it elevated on the surrounding bars of the lighthouse. Nearly a month before, in this same spot, I asked Hailey Thomas to marry me. She is in Cancun, Mexico for her sister's wedding. I am supposed to fly out tomorrow evening.

I closed my eyes to remember the excitement in hers, the moment she said yes to my proposal, and wondered about her inevitable disappointment when I don't walk off that plane. What would she be thinking when the flight attendant calls for final boarding and I'm not standing there next to her. I hope she was more worried than upset. It is better that she does not know about Rose or the shooting. I know she will understand what happened when the time is right.

An hour passed and I watched darkness follow the sunset and blanket the surrounding seascape. I tried to relax and focus on what needed to happen with Chase Anderson in the morning. The silence lasted a long time before the noise from a car engine interrupted my thoughts. It sputtered to a faint roar that gave way to the roll of the incoming tide. I listened until the car was gone and stood with all my weight on one leg as the large light bulbs began to brighten behind me and stepped inside through the open window and walked down the narrow steps. The first floor had an open room without furniture and limited décor.

Large windowpanes surrounded me as I slowly walked through the entranceway and locked the door before placing the key underneath the conch shell behind the white rocking chair on the front porch.

The road was dark, and I limped in the shadows of streetlamps without thinking about the pain. Kevin probably waited for the incoming tide and got a late start tarpon fishing. Just being out on the water eased Kevin's nerves, and tonight without Rose in his life, a bottle of green label was probably as necessary as fishing.

* * *

Hailey Thomas stood in front of the Pedro Island lighthouse, sea oats bending under distant thunderclouds over neighboring Cayo Costa Island. Her keen eyes complimented long flowing hair and an inviting smile that could make me vulnerable in an instant. I tossed the black and white photograph of her on my desk and leaned back in my chair.

The .35-millimeter camera hung from the metal window crank. I grabbed it and looked through the lens as my editor, Dudas, walked toward me. I twisted the enormous man into focus.

"I'm sorry about what happened. Good thing Hailey's not around for this," Dudas said.

He wore an oversized button-down shirt with the collar tight around the base of a full beard and smoked the usual morning cigar. Beach cars with wood moldings and surf boards stretched in patterns across the shirt.

"He drove me home yesterday evening," I said. "I haven't seen him since."

"Is he out fishing?"

"Probably, but he didn't say. We're meeting with Chase Anderson in an hour."

"Again, Sands? Didn't you go through everything yesterday? And why are you dressed like a landscaper? Did you sleep outside last night?"

I looked down at my damp red t-shirt and dirt-stained khaki pants. I forgot where I left my flip-flops. Purple grease lines ran down my right leg from where I laid for cover under Kevin's truck during the shooting.

"At least comb your hair and wash your face. Maybe change clothes before you meet with him. He has an enormous influence over your next twenty years. You weren't made for prison, Butch. Trust me on this one."

I stood and walked over to the bathroom and splashed cold water over my face and matted hair. I looked at myself in the mirror and tried to remember why I decided to come into the office this morning. The work could wait. Helping Kevin and clearing my name were more important than island news. But I was drawn to work. Writing made life normal, if even for an hour this morning.

"And what's this?" Dudas asked. "Why do you have a plane ticket?"

"I'm supposed to fly to Mexico this evening. Remember?"

The plane ticket was taped to my computer monitor. Dudas leaned down and pushed his prescription glasses over his wide nose to read it.

"Today? I thought Hailey was flying you down there next week."

"No, she wants me there tonight."

"You can't leave today."

"Not if I want to clear my name. Besides, I can't leave Kevin right now."

"How'd she take the news that you're not coming?"

"Haven't told her yet. I wanted to call her from Miami but waited. Thought I had a chance to finish things with Chase. Thought I'd be packing for vacation this morning."

I grabbed the worn baseball from my desk and gripped it for a slider, lost for words.

"Are you serious? How can you—"

"Kevin needs me. I've never seen him like this. If I leave for two weeks, he'll do something I can't fix, ever."

"And the first ten years of your marriage may be spent in prison if you don't fix this with the Miami PD. Chase Anderson knows a lot about what happened. He really believes you're hiding money."

"Can you be the one person that doesn't need to ask me about the money? I need you to just trust me."

Dudas sighed and walked to the kitchen with an empty coffee mug. I turned and watched the blinking cursor below a jumble of words on the computer monitor. Dudas was back within seconds, staring at me with a peculiar look.

"You know you're lucky to still have this job. You haven't written anything of substance for over a month."

"You remind me of that once a week."

"How? I haven't had you for an entire week in months. I hate to admit it, but our readers miss you."

I smiled at the backhanded compliment and stood up from the desk. We were eye level now. He raised the steaming mug between us and drank.

"Hailey needs me. Chase Anderson needs me. Kevin needs me but won't admit it. You need me. Readers need me."

"Feels good to be needed, right Sands?"

"I just want Kevin to get through this without ruining his own life. Hailey will understand when she knows why—"

"What should I tell her, Butch? I'll step in for you."

"Seriously, you'd do that?"

For a moment, I found solace in my loud, demanding and overanxious editor. This reminded me why my late father was so loyal to him and this newspaper.

"Tell her I love her and I'm sorry. Tell her Kevin needs me more than ever and that I'll see her in a week and make it up to her."

"I think I can relay that message."

Dudas looked down at his watch. He rolled his eyes and shook his melon-sized head.

"Thanks, Dudas."

"Oh, almost forgot to ask you about that tarpon fishing story. The fishing guides association is expecting something to be printed this week. They're taking the jig captains to court next month."

"I'm the one who pushed for that story in the first place. Believe me, the guides have reminded me enough about it," I said. "I'm practically finished. I just need to read it through a few more times."

"Remember, we're talking livelihood here."

"I'll just give it to Carla for a proof-read before I go.

It's probably fine the way it is."

"I'd prefer that."

I leaned over my keyboard and quickly saved the open article and sent it to Carla's printer. It felt good to finish something for print.

"What's more important than our livelihood?" I said under my breath.

Dudas let out an aching cough followed by a wheezing sound as the laser jet printer pushed the three pages through. Before Carla could check, Dudas had to waddle around her desk. He pulled the pages off the printer. After one more gulp of steaming black coffee, he turned toward me. I felt my vibrating cell phone and reached for it. It was Chase Anderson, but I sent him to voicemail.

"Are we good now, Dudas?"

"We're good. The association will appreciate your story. Now go on and save yourself and Kevin. Then come back safe."

Dudas flicked cigar ash into the conch shell on Carla's desk and walked through the unusually quiet newsroom to his corner office and shut the door. I knew the Tarpon story would help our tarpon fishery and tossed the baseball back in the desk drawer and refocused on the seaplane pictures for Chase Anderson.

* * *

Broken shells absorbed the scorching heat on Palm Avenue. Coconut palms that lined the grassy medium through the center of town looked thirsty with dead palm fronds bending down and away from the sun. A few locals walked along the clean sidewalks. Tourist season was dead for now. Only workers, day-trippers and year-round residents stayed for the unpleasant end of summer.

I walked across the street toward the rusted yellow truck that sat absorbing the morning sun. The canopy of Marker 17 Tavern blocked the sunlight. I opened the driver's side door, and stopped at the sight of Joe, the owner and lone bartender.

"Where you headed, Butch?" Joe asked.

"Looking for Kevin. Have you seen him?"

"You know he's out chasing tarpon. Why do you ask?"

"I know, just thought he'd be easy for once and we could be on time for this meeting."

"Meeting? Business?"

"Far from that."

"Hey, Peabody said something about you flying to Mexico to see Hailey."

"Supposed to meet up with her but can't get away from my past long enough to even enjoy a vacation."

I noticed Joe was wearing a wet kitchen apron. He usually made a few drinks in the evenings just to visit with locals but never did anything else.

"Are you washing dishes?"

"Help is scarce right now. I'm practically the cook too."

"I understand that."

"Why haven't you been around lately, Butch?"

"I know. I miss your pan seared snapper too."

"Well, if you write good enough storylines, I'll understand. We're all busy."

"I haven't seen Peabody much either. How's he been?"

"He started drinking again. Captain Dan keeps him busy though. Kevin will charter for Captain Dan this fall, right?"

"I'm not sure. He's supposed to spend most of November in Denver."

"Colorado's nice. God, I remember fishing the White River. What a perfect river. And the trout were nice, too." Joe took a long drag from the cigarette and wiped the sweat from his forehead with the bottom of his apron. His eyes looked tired.

"Kevin says the White River is the best kept secret in Colorado. On a bad day, he will catch twenty or so white fish and a few rainbows."

"Yeah, he's the reason I went there in the first place. By the way, we haven't seen you out on the pass lately. Don't tell me you're too busy for fishing too?"

I thought about the fly-tie vice clamped on the corner of my desk collecting dust. I remember tying my first La Tarpon fly, black eye inside a yellow head with the flowing white and orange tail, and wished I were sitting there now, working on a few different patterns with the sunrise below the cracked seawall and rising tide.

"I miss it."

"You know, Kevin and I trolled for Spanish mackerel last week. Kevin brought us into a school. I landed a fifty pounder. Think it was nearly six—"

"Sorry, Joe, what time is it?"

"Almost seven thirty."

"Hell, the sun isn't even up yet."

"Go if you need to, Butch. I won't hold you up."

"Thanks. Hey, I submitted that culinary piece to the Sarasota and Tampa newspapers. Maybe that will bring some more business?"

"I know you did. Thanks for that," Joe said and lit another cigarette. "Where have you been the past few weeks? You still trying to clear your name with that dead banker's widow in New York?"

"Yeah, now something happened to Kevin's girl—"

"I know about Rose. Kevin was in here for three hours last night. Never seen someone drink that much scotch on an empty stomach. Poor bastard is devastated. He loved her."

"What did he say—"

The front screen door shot open, and a crowd of locals hurried inside. One of the men dressed in a navy-blue suit pulled Joe inside with them. Joe made a gesture for me to wait for a minute but there was no time.

Chapter Four

I sat across from Kevin inside Leo's, a shoebox diner with pale-green walls and vintage pictures of boats and fishermen standing beside tarpon and other prominent game fish, all of them smiling with black and white backgrounds. The short order cook was an older gray-haired woman, who was Leo's widow. She smoked a corncob pipe on her breaks and was known for making the best omelets in Southwest Florida.

Leo's Diner was Kevin's favorite place to eat, but today, he sat with sad eyes and sulking shoulders. His western omelet sat untouched on the table between us. I ate the last piece of sausage on my plate and sat back against the cushioned booth and decided to break the comfortable silence we shared since leaving Pedro Island that morning.

"You haven't eaten in two days, Kev."

"So, what. I can't think about food right now. When is this guy showing up? He's an hour late."

I turned to look at the parking lot just as an unmarked police cruiser pulled in next to our yellow truck. Chase Anderson jogged across the gravel lot and walked inside the diner.

"Hit rush-hour traffic, Butch," Chase said.

"No problem. Have a seat. This is my brother, Kevin." Chase shook Kevin's hand and sat down next to me.

He smelled like cigar smoke and his clothes were wrinkled. Kevin was noticeably uncomfortable and shifted in his seat just as Chase tossed an open pack of cigarettes on the table and leaned forward. He looked at me first then at Kevin.

"I know you must be devastated. Our department has been tracking—"

"What do you know so far?" Kevin asked. "You don't know how the waiting feels."

Chase sat back and reached for the pack of cigarettes. He packed the soft box on the heel of his palm and offered one to Kevin.

"I know this is hard, Kevin. But your cooperation can only help this case."

I watched Kevin light his cigarette and take a long drag before exhaling a lazy smile. He looked anxious and hopeless at the same time. I knew his insides were churning.

"This case is my life. I thought this guy has been on your radar for years. Who else did he murder?"

Chase exhaled and looked at the older couple behind our table. He cleared his throat and rubbed his tan forehead. He seemed hesitant to speak.

"My wife . . . two years ago this coming Sunday," Chase said.

Kevin froze. I turned to watch his reaction. I was stunned.

"Tatum Jones murdered your wife?" I asked.

"No one knows if he pulled the trigger. But his cell number was the last to call her phone."

Kevin rubbed his tired eyes and gave me a blank stare. I knew what he was thinking without saying a word. He did not know about the deal I made with Chase and the seaplane photographs.

"You have the pictures, Butch?" Chase asked. "You brought them, right?"

"In the truck. We'll get to them last."

"Last? Only reason I'm here . . . check that, only reason you're not waking up in county jail is because of those photos."

"What do you know about Tatum Jones?" Kevin asked. "I need an address, phone number, anything."

I was surprised at Kevin's bluntness. His style was usually less aggressive. Chase smirked at the question and leaned back to blow smoke rings over the table. White rings rose above his unkempt blonde hair.

"If I knew any of those things, why would I need you guys? Tatum Jones has about fifty addresses, about seventy-five cell numbers, and probably twenty bastard children that we know about in Greater Miami alone. What would you do with that information? Don't think for a second that I'd give something like that up to you without visiting him in person first."

"Sounds like I'd do what you can't do."

I felt the tension mounting between them. Both had lost everything because of one dealer. If I didn't mediate soon this would be a waste of everyone's time. Not to mention, I'd be back in Chase's office answering questions again with my lawyer taking notes.

"Kev, walk with me for a minute," I said.

"Why?"

I grabbed Kevin by the arm and pulled him up then started pushing him ahead of me toward the front door. Chase Anderson sat back and looked at a menu.

"Getting your pictures," I said, glancing back at Chase.

"I'll be right here," Chase said and took a bite of Kevin's omelet.

I followed Kevin to the truck and waited for him to talk first. He leaned over the rusted bed and dropped his head down. Sunlight pushed shadows across the parking lot in front of us.

"Do you believe him?" Kevin asked. "Think he really lost his wife?"

"Yeah, I believe him, and I think we can help each other."

"I understand why we need this guy, Butch, believe me. But my insides are shot, and I don't feel anything anymore. I can't do anything until Tatum Jones is dead."

The humidity fell over us like a blanket. I understood why Kevin was acting this way. But the last thing I ever wanted to see was my brother transform into a thoughtless killer.

"I know you're frustrated. But remember the people who care about you. Life in prison is nothing to take lightly."

"Who said anything about prison?"

Kevin looked up at me with bloodshot eyes. The sight of him crying floored me. I stopped thinking and tried to hold back my own emotions. Nothing in life prepares you for losing someone you love more than you love yourself. We were always more than just brothers. The first time I remember knowing him, he took time to show me things, even let me run around with him and his older friends.

"Maybe Chase can help. We should let the police help us. There are ways to punish him without—"

"No, Butch. I'm not letting him live in prison until drug money gets him paroled in five years."

"How do you know that?"

"How do you not?"

I could see his mind was made up and there was nothing I could say to change it. I turned to look at Chase through the front window. He sat watching us.

"What's your plan, then?"

Kevin held on to the side of the truck-bed and leaned back to stretch his round shoulders. He turned to look at me with the same half smile I had grown accustomed to when something was about to change.

"I'm leaving. This situation is better without me."

"How will I get back?"

Kevin pointed toward Chase and smiled. He opened the driver side door and got in. The truck was backing out before I could react.

"Hold up, Kev!"

The truck came to a quick stop. Kevin leaned out the window as he lit a cigarette. He was still fighting emotion.

"Get your name cleared with Miami PD first," Kevin said. "If those pictures help your situation . . . great. That's important to you and me."

"What about Tatum Jones?"

"I'll find him," Kevin said. "Let me do this alone. Hailey needs you alive."

The truck roared out of the small parking lot and turned Northbound toward the highway. I watched the faded yellow tailgate move along the on-ramp and disappear in the distant line of heat and humidity.

Chapter Five

Chase drove the unmarked police cruiser through and around traffic while Frank Sinatra sang at an uncomfortably loud volume. He had not asked for directions to Pedro Island yet and neither of us talked since leaving the diner. I held on to the hand rest as we sped around a charter bus along the grassy median and bounced back inside the fast lane. A worn baseball rolled beneath my feet on the floorboard. I reached down and picked it up. Chase turned the music down and looked at me like I was a stranger.

"Where'd you find that? Thought I lost it."

The smooth cowhide covering and raised stitching calmed my nerves. Chase looked concerned about something.

"You know where you're going?"

"Sure. I've been to Pedro Island a few times before. The exit isn't for another ten miles or so, right?"

Chase reached over with his free hand and grabbed the baseball. He looked at it for a time then went back to driving. He was calm again.

"What about Tatum Jones? You have the pictures. Are we going to talk about it?"

He leaned back in his seat and sighed. The subject was unavoidable and the only reason we met this morning. My trust for Chase was beginning to fade. I knew Kevin thought Chase was a liability.

"What's there to talk about? Consider yourself lucky that you have a journalist's mentality. Those pictures are the only reason you didn't spend last night in a Miami jail."

"Okay, I understand that part. What about Rose? My brother?"

"You both need to have patience right now. Even if your brother wanted to find Tatum . . . let's just say winning the power ball lottery is better odds."

"Have you ever met him?"

Chase cleared his throat and set the baseball in the center console. Reaching over the visor, he pulled down a pack of cigarettes, and steered with a knee as he lit one. Two quick inhales followed a long exhale that filled the empty back seat and lingered with the windows up. I powered my window down and a warm rush of air blew my hair back.

"I'd rather not talk about it with you, Butch. Rose is one of a hundred open felony cases involving Tatum Jones."

"You didn't answer my question."

"Look, I want to help your brother . . . but information is classified for a reason and the Chief would have my ass if I gave it—"

"My brother's girlfriend was just murdered in broad daylight. And it appears you're not high on Chief Digg's list now. Are we going to help each other or not?"

He sighed and looked at me with seriousness in his eyes that had not been there before. Everything seemed loose or no big deal to Chase until now. Maybe he had something important to tell me.

"Look, you know I have something in common with your brother. If one word gets out about these pictures or us meeting this morning, you'll spend the next month locked up in county jail on suspicion alone. Understand?"

I was surprised at the openness and nodded yes. Chase took another drag off the cigarette and turned hard to cut off a pickup truck and exited the interstate earlier than he was supposed to exit.

"Where are we going?"

"Do you understand? The chief will fire me on the spot."

"Yes, I understand. But why did you exit?"

"Want to show you something."

We passed a lone gas station toward an intersection with train tracks. Chase slowed the cruiser and turned right on a dirt road. He sped through palm trees and overgrown palmettos toward an abandoned stilt house at the end of the road. The cruiser came to a sliding stop. Chase got out and started to walk away. I jumped out and followed.

"Grace was murdered five years ago. Tatum ruined my life without knowing it," Chase said. "He's a monster that needs to be stopped."

"Didn't you say it was a speculation that Tatum murdered Grace?"

"Sure, but she's still gone because of him."

I stood facing him with sand and dust settling around our feet. He was breathing heavy now with a backdrop of coconut palms leaning over a seawall ten yards away. He gripped the baseball and held it against his right thigh as he leaned over just enough to read a phantom catcher's sign.

"Were you a pitcher, Chase?"

He nodded and turned to throw a fastball that bounced off one of the nearby coconut palms. This question seemed to have incensed Chase even more.

"I need a few minutes," he said, as he started jogging over to find the baseball in a cluster of palmettos and walked toward the seawall.

I sat on the hood of the cruiser and thought about Kevin and where he was right now. The meeting this morning may have saved me from jail, but it did nothing for Kevin and his pursuit of Tatum Jones. I needed to get home and find him . . . protect him from himself.

"What are you showing me, Chase? Whose house is this?"

He ignored my question and sat down on the cracked concrete wall. Shoulders sulked and his head fell forward. Something about this place triggered his emotions. I decided to add urgency to the situation and walked over to sit down next to him.

"Why did you bring me here? I'm sorry about what happened to you, but my brother needs me right now and we—"

Chase looked over at me with red eyes. He tightened his square jaw and nodded. I looked down at the brackish water and spotted a school of mullet circling a lone piling where a dock once stood.

"That's my house," Chase said. "This is my land."

"Looks abandoned—"

"Grace and I had plans to start our life there."

Overgrown shrubs filled in the open spaces between scattered palmettos. An acre of thick mangroves blocked the south side where five sabal palms stood together.

"It has to be hard to come here," I said. "Are you going to finish?"

"Not without her. I look at it as motivation. Sure, some developer will come in here one day and bulldoze it to the ground, maybe build multiple condos and dredge this canal for commercial fishing boats to berth. But we bought it together. Two weeks later, she's dead. Wasn't ready to give it up then. It's complicated now."

"No doubt. This is a great property."

A blue scrub jay landed on his shoulder. I sat back, surprised that a wild bird was this fearless. Chase calmly reached over and let the bird jump on his hand.

"The good news in all of this is that no one is going to build anything else on this property anytime soon."

"Why not?"

"A month after she died, the original landowner called to let me know I could never build a house or even a boat dock because scrub jays are a protected species in Florida. But as you can see, we were well into it by then."

The scruffy bird pecked at his open palm then flew away. Chase looked up at the sabal palms and smiled.

"Ironic. I own a skeleton stilt house and two meaningless waterfront acres."

"Why did you bring me here?"

He stood from the seawall and pulled another cigarette from the soft pack in his shorts pocket and lit it. I stood to face him.

"I want Tatum Jones as badly as Kevin wants him. This place reminds me of what I'm fighting for . . . what he took from me. This stop was more for me than you. But I wanted you to know that I'm fully committed to this . . . and you can trust that I'm not telling you this for the sake of conversation. This is real, Butch."

I stepped back as he exhaled smoke. My first impression of Chase Anderson was anything but positive. The loud, arrogant rookie cop with something to prove was someone Kevin and I needed now. He was an asset with a common purpose.

I know Kevin wants to find Tatum alone. Chase will have to prove he is trustworthy to us in his own way. Kevin will eventually understand why he needs Chase more than he needs us.

* * *

Chase Anderson slowed the cruiser as we approached Tarpon Marina, the only marina on Pedro Island. We stopped before an unnamed boat that rested on blocks behind the fueling pumps. I got out and stood at the window.

"What now?" I asked.

"Forget we ever met this morning, Butch," Chase said. "I'll personally deliver those pictures to my guy at the lab. Should know something in a day or . . . if not sooner."

Kevin could be halfway to the Florida Keys by now, chasing his own lead for Tatum Jones. A day was too long. I turned to scan the docks in search of him or his boat. He was not here.

"Sooner is better. Kevin is on a mission."

"Write your cell number on this."

Chase handed me a pen and an empty cracker box. I wrote both my cell and office number on the label and handed it back to him. He looked at it and tossed the box on the passenger side floorboard where the baseball was rolling at my feet.

"Be available to talk around six or so," Chase said.

"Which number?"

I watched the cruiser speed away and turn down a side road then turned to face the inactive marina. A forty-foot Cape Dory Explorer, navy-blue hull with twin diesel engines, sat on blocks behind the bait coolers. The owner was from New Jersey but had not been back for three years now. He was a broker that paid for its berth on time, every month. I knew it was one of five ever built and hoped it was for sale. Of course, I couldn't afford the two hundred-thousand-dollar price. That is, unless I used some of the money buried on Cayo Costa Island.

"I always catch you staring at her, Butch," a familiar voice said.

I looked over at Hash, a sixty something shark fisherman, sitting in the bow of his home. *Willey's Hooker* was in black letters beneath his bare feet.

"How's it going, Hash?"

"Fine. You find some new friends?"

"No, just gave me a ride."

"Sure, they did." Hash smiled. "She's for sale, you know."

The lanky man chewed tobacco and wiped his filthy hands with a rag. I noticed the shark blood smeared across the wooden deck of his thirty-foot center console.

"I didn't know that."

"They found her owner hanging from his basement pull-up bar in Jersey. Heard he lost millions on hedge funds. Owed everybody money."

"That's too bad. Did you know him?"

"Only met him one time, the very day he brought her here. Always paid his bills but he never came around.

"I heard that about him."

"She's in rough shape though. Damn fine trawler once. I think the original owner ran her into a sand bar and left her for dead. No name either. Never seen that before, boat without a name."

Hash stood from a fighting chair and stuffed the rag in the pocket of his stained overalls and jumped up on the dock. He smiled and walked over to shake my hand and spit a black stream of tobacco on a pink hibiscus flower.

"Wanted to thank you for that Tarpon article. That meant a lot to us, the ones who depend on this fishery for our livelihood, anything to shine a spotlight on those jig captain parasites coming down from Tampa and St. Pete with their big outboards. Most of them have never heard of long-drifting for tarpon."

"No problem. I'd like to see less of them as well."

"You look nothing like your brother, Kevin. Where in the hell did you come from anyway?"

I smiled at the comment. Kevin and I look like distant cousins at best. Our late father, James, used to say I was the milkman's child.

"You should come out with me for a shark charter. Kevin always tells me you're too busy . . . especially lately. Nothing like wrangling a hammerhead."

"Yeah, I've heard. Have you talked to Kevin today?"

"Not today or a week for that matter. Why?"

I knew he had no idea about Rose's death. No one on the island could have known yet. I decided to keep it to myself and cut this short.

"I need to go, Hash. Kevin and I have something—"

"Sure. Remember, if you're looking to hunt sharks, I'm your guy. Many a night I've fished for sharks on the pass with your father. He was a great writer, too."

"I know. He used to tell me stories when I was a kid."

"Maybe you and Dudas could come out one night?"

The sun was the centerpiece of a cloudless sky, and the asphalt was heating up around us. Hash ran his index finger along his gum line and scooped chewing tobacco from his mouth and tossed it against one of the dock cleats.

"I'll ask Dudas about it."

"Do that. I'll check my upcoming schedule."

"What's the asking price for this boat by the way?"

I walked along the navy-blue hull of the trawler toward the bow then underneath to the starboard side. The nameless boat spoke to my heart. I wanted to drop it today and cruise at fifteen knots south toward the Florida Keys.

"Better question for Vince."

"Is he working today?"

"What's today? Is today a weekday?"

"It's Friday."

"He should be around the sales office then."

"I'll catch up with him next week," I said and noticed the time on his watch. "Tell him I'm interested if you see him."

"Will do. Hope to see you hammerhead hunting soon."

"Set up a time with Dudas. I'll go anytime."

I turned to walk away across the lot and imagined the twin diesel engines pushing against the Gulf Stream, a newly painted turquoise hull, white deck, and Hailey lying outstretched on the stern with nothing but the deep blue water behind us.

Chapter Six

Sunlight cast shadows along Palm Avenue. I walked across the empty road and hurried inside the *Island Courier* building. Kevin was still missing, and another day of uncertainty was nearing its end.

The messy newsroom was quiet. I expected Dudas to be working late as usual, but his office was dark. I walked over to my computer without turning on any lights and began to search my documents. I stopped after a few minutes and sat back in my chair to read a ten-year-old story my late father had written about funding support for causeway repairs. Piles of paperwork sat in front of me. I thought about Hailey and the clear blue surf in Cancun. Being with her in a normal situation seemed impossible. I just wanted to be comfortable and still, with her. I needed Kevin back, tying flies for an upcoming charter, smoking cigarettes at our grandfather's hutch inside his bungalow with slow rolling waves outside the open crank windows.

A door slammed to break the silence. Dudas hurried in with Carla, nodded at me then walked inside the big corner office. He was sweating and noticeably in a good mood.

"How's the leg, Sands?" Dudas asked.

"Better," I said and stood from my chair to check the bandage on my leg. I walked gingerly around Carla toward his office.

"Any messages, Carla?"

"Hailey must have sent this next day," Carla said and handed me an envelope.

"Thanks," I said and put the envelope in my pocket.

"Come on in, Sands," Dudas said.

I entered the big office and closed the door behind me. The large tarpon hung on the wall behind the desk. Every time I looked up at the hundred and forty-pound fish, it created urgency inside me, and I wanted to call Kevin and drop everything in search of another, bigger tarpon.

Dudas cleared his throat and began to pull from a crooked pile of paperwork. He had marked up several pages with blue highlighter. I knew his routine and guessed his agenda was for me to write a new, big story.

"What did the doc say, Butch?"

"Just a graze. It's fine."

"Good. Now about Tatum Jones," Dudas said and continued to highlight sentences. "Ninety-one, assault; ninety-two, possession, six kilos of cocaine; ninety-six, possession of stolen property, illegal aliens, and counterfeit money; same year, impersonating a police officer; the list continues. And these are only the convicted cases. God knows how many more he has pending."

Dudas looked up from the blue highlighted lines. His plump red cheeks pushed up against his beady eyes when he smiled.

"How about a story on this guy?"

"Story? He killed Kevin's girlfriend and almost killed me. But no one knows this yet. The Miami PD is investigating him."

I knew I shouldn't have said it after I said it. Rose was like an adopted niece to Dudas. Her parents lived two houses down from him, on the South side of Pedro Island. He never married nor had any kids. He went to Rose's soccer games, gave to school fund raisers for her teams, even helped her find a few colleges.

"I know that Rose is dead," Dudas said and pointed down at an obituary article from the Miami Herald. "She's the unidentified female victim."

"Yes. Look, I'm sorry—"

"I thought you went to Miami alone. Where was Kevin?"

"They insisted on driving me down. We had no idea—"

"How could you have known? Forget about the other stories you've been working on for now. Just listen to me."

Dudas stood up and chucked the highlighter across the room and crossed both chubby arms in frustration. A long silence followed before he sat back in his big leather chair and lowered his head. His smile was gone, and plump cheeks completely covered his eyes for a second.

"This is a big one. I don't know how to tell Jake and Tina about Rose?"

"Don't say anything yet. Only Kevin and I know about her."

Dudas had no idea about Chase Anderson. He knew nothing about our agreement to help him and keep me away from litigation. He would undoubtedly argue against protecting Chase Anderson in pursuit of Rose's killer. His demeanor was sad yet alive with anger.

"I'll call Jake and—"

"You can't do that. Let the Miami PD handle it."

"But Jake's my best friend . . . that's his only daughter."

"Kevin has completely lost all reason for living since it happened. He loved Rose, I mean *really loved her*. And now he wants revenge."

"I understand, Butch. I do know about investigations and how the court of public reason can tip a killer off, allowing him to run. But this won't be easy. Where's Kevin?"

"No idea."

"You need to find him before—"

"I know. Please, for our safety, don't be the one to tell her parents."

Dudas stood again and walked out of the office. He returned with a steaming ceramic cup of coffee. His red eyes were glazed over. The tarpon on the wall caught his attention.

"You are so much like your father. Has anyone ever told you that?"

"You and my mom always remind me."

"I know what James Sands would do next. But you need to remember that this guy nearly killed you. Remember that James also chased a killer . . . and neither of us wants that outcome again. I promised your mother that you'd be safe here. That I would ensure the same sort of thing wouldn't ever kill you."

"Trust me on this one, Dudas."

"You're in a perfect situation to bring Tatum Jones down. But he's connected beyond our imagination down there. No way you and Kevin can chase him without help. I'm pretty sure his operation goes up the coast to Tampa, maybe farther into the panhandle. Your words could bring him down."

I knew where this was going and decided to tell him about Chase Anderson. Dudas was trustworthy and would be a necessary ally. He has been a father figure since my dad died a few years ago.

"I spent three hours with a rookie detective named Chase Anderson. We met after the shooting."

"He's the one you met with about your kidnapping."

"Right. They think I'm hiding money from the family in New York. He wanted to press charges on the spot. But we made an agreement."

"What agreement? Can't wait for this one."

"What it comes down to is the fact that I took pictures of the shooter's get away seaplane. They believe it belongs to Tatum Jones."

"James would've done the same thing."

"Chase has his own personal history with Tatum Jones. He was supposedly involved in his wife's murder years ago and is the reason Chase became a cop."

"That's amazing. Another twist in the story."

"He's been after Tatum Jones since day one but has never gotten close. That rap-sheet you just read from is the tip of the iceberg with this guy."

"Why do you think he gets away with everything? Is he connected with the Miami PD maybe?"

"I don't know. But illusive is an understatement."

Dudas began to pace. He stopped to set the coffee mug down and rubbed chubby palms together. A stack of papers caught his attention, and the sadness was gone. He was an editor again.

"I know how he does it. Money. The green backs. Guy probably pulls thirty grand on a slow day. Figure he pays out about five to ten for victims and witnesses to keep quiet. Hush money, you know. A couple thousand is gold to those people."

"Those people?"

"There's more to this story than you know. I spent a few hours last night researching this guy," Dudas said and raised both eyebrows. "What about his boss, this other guy, Chief Diggs? You know he's dirty, right?"

"What? How do you know that?"

"I've known that for years. Your father knew that back when he covered the cane workers in Dade County. Yeah, Diggs is in his position because of Tatum Jones."

"Seriously? How are they affiliated?"

"First off, when you first said the name Tatum Jones, did he act different?"

"As opposed to a normal reaction. How would I know? I've never met the guy before."

"Here's the short of it. Tatum has been running things in Miami for most of the nineties, cocaine back and forth from Miami to Columbia, money laundering, undocumented immigrant importation, stolen money, stolen seaplanes, you name it. Bastards got a fleet of seaplanes up and down the coast." Dudas pointed to a legal document crowded with blue highlighter. "Sonuvabitch escaped prison in Frankfurt,

Kentucky, with the help of his prostitute girlfriend, Brianna Coles, and started breaking the law as soon as he moved to Miami where he stole his first seaplane."

"What about Chief Diggs?"

"Filthy," Dudas said as he removed half the stack and placed it on the floor next to his chair. "Here, it's all right here in your father's notes." His fingers walked down page after page of blue highlighter. "Too much to get into right now. Let's just say, Diggs is deep in Tatum's pocket. And your rookie cop friend has no clue." Dudas leaned over the paperwork with a wide smile. "But we're going to tell him."

"How long has this been going on?"

"Twenty years at minimum."

"Why haven't you done anything before now?"

"Needed an edge. And you witnessing Tatum Jones in the act is exactly the edge I needed." Dudas picked up the phone. "Carla, can you arrange a lunch with Detective Chase Anderson with the Miami PD? Make it for the Blue Crab, tomorrow afternoon. Thank you, dear."

"This is unbelievable."

"One more thing. Do you have digital copies of the seaplane pictures?"

"Sure. But if I agree to do this, you need to pull back some and stop micro-managing me. Especially on this story. I need your complete and total trust."

"That's fair. It seems you have proven yourself to this point. You can also use the expense account for this story. Now, go find Kevin before he does something he'll regret. I'll call you tomorrow morning about lunch with Chase Anderson."

"Fine."

I stood from the desk and walked out of the office. Carla sat talking on the phone. She motioned for me to wait.

"I have a message for you," she said and covered the phone. "Your brother called just a few minutes ago."

"Where was he?" I asked.

"Said to meet him at home as soon as possible."

I was instantly relieved he had called and wanted to run home. My aching leg slowed me down the front steps, but I ignored the pain and jogged along Palm Avenue past Marker 17 Tavern and the row of yellow streetlamps that stood at the four-way intersection. Darkness fell on the island as I ran parallel with the old phosphate railway line and thought about the bullets that just missed me. A sense of mortality followed, and I began to sprint.

Chapter Seven

I jogged down the shell filled driveway that led to the bungalow I shared with Kevin. The lights were on and I opened the door to head inside but hesitated at the sight of Kevin smoking a pipe and cleaning a gun.

"Why are you sweating, Butch?" Kevin asked.

"I ran here. What are you doing with the shotguns?"

Kevin kept his focus on the black shiny barrel of our grandfather's 12-gauge. Two .44 magnums rested on the kitchen table on top of cleaning rags. He gripped the shotgun with one hand and held an open bottle of Outers 445 gun oil with the other hand.

"Cleaning them," Kevin said with a bearded smile. "What does it look like?"

"Whatever. I thought you were—"

"Been here since noon."

He could have been dead for all I knew, but here he was cleaning guns at the kitchen table. I walked past him, frustrated beyond reason, and went into the bathroom. The cool water felt good on my face and matted hair. I looked back at my eyes and felt like I was looking at a stranger. The mirror reminded me that stress and lack of sleep were taking their toll. I took in a few deep breaths and walked out to confront Kevin about Tatum Jones.

"Dudas knows about Rose," I said, expecting the reaction I saw.

Kevin stopped cleaning and looked up at me, wide-eyed. I waited for him to talk first. He calmly set the gun down and pulled a pouch of pipe tobacco from the front pocket of his fishing overalls. He packed the corncob pipe with the precision of a surgeon. I watched him hold the lighter at an angle and light a fire. He held steady until a cloud of smoke lifted past his dark beard and long hair that covered his eyes.

"Why say anything about Rose?" Kevin exhaled a plume of smoke in my direction. "Especially that loudmouth."

"Dudas was a second father to Rose."

"I know that."

"We need to think about this thing. You aren't the only one looking for Tatum Jones. Rose is the latest in a long line of victims."

"No. She stops the line. He won't get to anyone else."

His confidence was real, and I was completely thrown off by his reaction to Dudas knowing about Rose. It seemed unrelated to anything he cared about. He clearly wanted to go solo on this, no different from any past adversities he faced. He even left for six months after our father was murdered a few years ago. Said he needed nature to calm his anger. Big sky country with his dogs and a stream dividing mountains. People were rarely his antidote for great loss and emotional pain. He had always been a maverick. Said he needed to be where the train tracks stopped, anywhere away from people and schedules.

"Dudas did some research on this guy. He has resources, some Miami PD, some Cuban, but mostly a heavily funded army always surrounds him."

"So, what. Where was his army when he blew up that gas station? I could've taken him out right then if I had these. It was just him and the pilot."

Kevin picked up the shotgun again and slammed it on the table. He stood up and said something under his breath. I froze and waited for him to talk again. The silence was uncomfortable.

"I know you have a life here," Kevin said. "I know you're following in dad's footsteps with Dudas and the newspaper . . . but I'm not you.

Never have been. I loved Rose. She's dead now, but that still means something to me. She understood me. I've never had that before."

I completely understood his stance and wanted to tell him that he was right. But the truth would only encourage him to pursue Tatum Jones on a suicide mission. He was still the brother worth fighting for and I could not lose him this way.

"I'm going for a walk," Kevin said. "Please don't follow me."

He adjusted the pipe and rubbed his beard in deep thought and walked toward the front door. I could not let him out of my sight in this condition and grabbed his shoulder.

"Let's have a few beers and talk about it. When's the last time we had a beer together at Marker 17 Tavern?"

He turned and nodded. I followed him outside and we walked along the same driveway I had just run down. This time, I was in no hurry to get anywhere. He offered me the corncob pipe and I took a long pull from it. Evening had set in on Pedro Island and a cool wind pushed through the yard and moved the hibiscus bushes away from the road. There was no moon and the sounding tide beat against the seawall as we passed Banyan Street.

Kevin opened the worn screen door and made his way inside Marker 17 Tavern. I followed him through a small crowd of locals gathered around a dark corner table near the large walk-in humidor. Kevin walked past them toward the bar and immediately found a seat. Older, pale skinned tourists and vacationing college students crowded the bar. Joe the bartender began to pour two pints of Guinness and motioned for me to see him at the end of the bar.

"Damn good to see you two together," Joe said.

"Yeah. I found him cleaning guns in the kitchen."

"Guns? Listen. I got a call from some Chase fellow about ten minutes ago. He asked for you by name," Joe said and handed me the two pints. "He said it was urgent and to keep you here for about an hour until he shows up."

"But how did he know?"

I realized that Chase had bugged our house. There was no other explanation for him knowing we were here. He was more of a professional than I originally thought.

Joe smiled at the sight of me holding pints inside his bar again, like old times, and patted me on the shoulder. It felt good to be home and around locals I'd known for a long time. The people I wrote for and about. It especially helped me temporarily forget about being without Hailey for another night.

"Kevin looks like a damn grizzly bear, doesn't he?" Joe shouted. "He's a bearded animal."

"Right," I said laughing. "Did Chase leave a number to call?"

"Nope. Said he'd just meet you right here."

"Thanks, Joe."

I slid a pint down to Kevin and found a seat next to him. The elk head stared at us from the wall behind the bar. A cigar hung from its partially opened mouth. Kevin ate peanuts from a wicker basket as he scanned the barroom.

"Chase is meeting us here in about an hour."

Kevin stopped eating and gave me a look of confusion. He took a long drink of the dark beer and set in on the bar before he crossed wide forearms.

"Is that why you—"

"I just found out from Joe. He called here and asked Joe to keep us around until he got here. Said it was urgent."

"I don't trust this guy."

"I didn't either at first, but I do now. We both need him for different reasons."

A small group of local fishermen rushed over toward us. They were drunk and acting the part. The skinny one wearing a Yankees hat tried to tackle Kevin off his barstool without success.

"Where you been, Kevin?" he asked as he backed away from the failed struggle. "You're either losing your touch out on the water or your reputation has finally run clients off. Which is it?"

Kevin reached for his pint and gave me a look of uncertainty. I leaned in and put my arm around his broad shoulders. Everything turned from rowdy to calm in a hurry. Silence did not fit Kevin's regular personality.

"I dragged him out tonight," I said. "He hasn't felt good all day but came anyway."

"Whatever, Butch. Quit covering for your older bro," one of them said from the crowd. "We'll leave princess alone tonight."

"Yeah," the skinny one said adjusting his hat. "He doesn't look ready for the title anyway. Make sure you tuck him in tonight, Butch."

The rowdy group moved away toward a group of ladies near the pool table. Kevin turned and motioned to Joe for two more pints. I scanned the room for Chase Anderson knowing it was too early for him to be here.

"Thanks, Butch. It's hard to fake it around that group. They live for two things, fishing hard and drinking hard."

"Maybe you'll be ready again in a week or so . . . once this whole thing is behind us."

Kevin pulled the corncob pipe and tobacco pouch out from the front pocket of his overalls and set them on the bar next to his pint glass. He lit a cigarette next and tossed the lighter on the bar between us.

"This will never be behind us," Kevin said. "Killing Tatum Jones doesn't bring Rose back. Nothing ever will."

Kevin looked away from me, probably to avoid seeing my reaction to his hopelessness. He waved at someone he recognized and stood from his barstool.

"Be right back," Kevin said. "Come get me if and when Chase shows up."

I sat back and watched him walk through the abundant crowd. Everyone knew him. Everyone touched him on the shoulders or tried to stop him from walking away from them. He turned and motioned for Joe to join him inside the giant humidor. I turned around on my barstool and held the pint in front of me.

"Butch Sands!"

I turned to see who was yelling my name. Chase Anderson stood in the entrance. We made eye contact, and he pushed through the rowdy group around the pool table and approached the bar. He was smiling big and laughing about something.

"Some of those women seem a little young for this place. Maybe I'm just getting too old for them." Chase had a toothpick stuck in his mouth. Dark sunglasses covered his eyes, and his black sport coat and black pants made him look out of place.

"Joe said an hour. It has been like ten minutes," I said. "Where did you come from?"

"Been outside for about five minutes talking to a couple of sophomores from Michigan." Chase motioned toward the door. "I have some added information on Tatum. Can we take a walk?"

"Sure," I said and finished my pint. "Should I get Kevin?"

Chase nodded and walked away through the crowd. I scanned the room for Kevin but didn't see him. The bar-back, Tuna, cleaned beer mugs near me.

"Tuna! Have you seen Kevin?"

"I passed him on my way in. He's smoking out front. What's going on with you, Butch? It's good to see you both in here. Been a while, right?"

"I know it has. Listen. I need to get to Kevin before something happens. Thanks again."

Tuna's expressions never changed. His tall lanky shape fit his calm and even-keel demeanor. He'd worn the same Pedro Outfitters hat and the same fishing vest since our first meeting during a fishing trip with our family about eight years earlier.

I rushed through the growing crowd and hurried outside. Kevin and Joe stood below a yellow streetlamp looking through a cigar box. They both looked up at me with raised eyebrows.

"Where's Chase?"

"It has only been ten minutes," Kevin said.

The familiar unmarked police cruiser pulled up behind Joe and Kevin and the passenger window lowered. Chase leaned over the center console and motioned for us to come inside. I hesitated and watched Kevin's reaction.

"Let's go, ladies," Chase said, "Bring your box."

Kevin closed the cigar box and shook his head at me. Joe appeared to sense the tension between us and calmly walked back inside his bar. I opened the door and sat down in the front seat. Kevin hesitated then walked around to the driver's side.

"I'm not going anywhere with you, Chase," Kevin said. "Nor do I need—"

"Get in the car," I said. "He has information about Tatum."

Kevin stepped back from a cloud of smoke and looked down the empty street.

"One of my undercover dealers spotted Tatum Jones this morning near South Beach," Chase said. "Tracked him to a house on Marathon Key. He's there now. No bullshit, Kevin."

"So why come to us? What about the Miami PD?"

Chase leaned back in his seat and held the black steering wheel. A cigarette burned down to the filter in the corner of his mouth. He looked at me then turned to lock eyes with Kevin.

"We all need something out of this. That's not even debatable," Chase finally said. "But we need each other too. I say we go after him, now while we have the chance. Call it irony or good luck. We never picked up his trail in the two months prior to the gas station shooting."

Kevin rubbed his beard and looked over the roof of the cruiser at a group of regulars walking past us on Palm Avenue. He held the cigar box to his side and leaned down to look at me. We made familiar eye contact, and our nonverbals took over. He finally shrugged and opened the door to join us. I nodded approval and motioned for Chase to drive away before Kevin changed his mind.

Chapter Eight

The crescent moon hung over Charlotte Harbor. I watched a narrow line of clouds that were stacked atop one another. A cool southeasterly wind bent palm trees that lined the low-tide bank and paralleled mangroves behind an empty fishing pier. Chase Anderson sat on the seawall smoking one of the prized cigars Kevin bought from Marker 17 Tavern just before we left.

Kevin appeared from mangrove darkness and walked toward the parked cruiser. I stood in the middle on a steep concrete bank and wondered whether Kevin trusted Chase or was using him for a way to find Rose's killer.

"I'm ready guys," Kevin said. "What is it, four to five hours?"

"Don't you think we should talk about this first?" I asked.

"He's right, Butch," Chase said. "We should leave and talk on the way."

Chase stood from his seawall perch and passed me with a trail of sweet cigar smoke that reminded me of my late grandfather. The cruiser started before I joined them inside it. I felt like a divorce lawyer around these two. Neither one had asked the other about anything personal. It was all business to this point.

"Can you both get off work for a few days?" Chase asked as he sped the cruiser over the long bridge that crossed the swirling Myakka River. "Your editor should be okay with that right, Butch?"

"Dudas should be okay with it, but he's waiting on a few unfinished stories from me."

"What's your schedule like, Kevin?" Chase asked.

"I just hope we make it to the Keys tonight. What's going to take a few days? Don't we have his location?"

Kevin turned his head and smiled. He lit another cigar from the box and shrugged at the unresponsive Chase. Finding Tatum Jones in the Keys was only half the risk tonight.

"What's the plan when we get there?" I asked.

"Come on, Butch," Chase said. "You're the one at risk here. Prison is no joke. And I'm up against two failed years of arresting one guy. Chief Diggs thinks I'm working South Beach on foot patrol tonight."

"So, we have no back up from Miami PD?"

"Listen, I could lose my job for what we're about to do and we all know why Kevin wants our mark."

The comment seemed to wake Kevin up from a trance. He leaned in toward Chase, cigar in mouth, and raised both eyebrows. I could feel the tension.

"So, why do I want Tatum Jones? Other than the obvious reason that he killed the love of my life?"

Chase took his eyes completely off the dark road ahead and matched Kevin's intensity. He glanced at me for a few seconds then went back to staring Kevin down. The cruiser suddenly came to a screeching stop, nearly slamming into a cluster of pine trees just over the shoulder.

"I know this is hard for you, but I lost someone too—"

"What does your life have to do with mine?"

Now that defeated look came back on his face. The same look Chase had when we sat on his abandoned waterfront property the day before. The same look when he told me about his dead wife and the life they were supposed to have led in that very place.

"Look, I understand what you're up against, Kevin. You're dealing with surmounting anger and sleepless nights. I still fight these same things, two years ago this Thursday, my wife was found dead. Tatum

Jones was the last person to call her cell. I've been chasing him ever since."

Kevin's head fell back on the seat rest, and he pulled at his beard the way he always did when uncertainty came. I waited for a reaction but only a long silence followed before he turned to look at me with wet eyes. He finally nodded approval and opened his door. I watched Chase's reaction as he stepped outside and walked away from the cruiser. Kevin got out next and walked in the opposite direction. Both were fighting similar emotions.

* * *

A horizontal line of lights shone across the pitch-black road. Chase throttled the unmarked cruiser along Alligator Alley and the dark green marsh of the Everglades. The constant secondhand cigar smoke and built-up adrenaline kept me from dozing off. Kevin had not said a word since finally agreeing to get back in the cruiser and join us again. His window was open, and I knew he was wide-awake.

"Your station is coming up," Chase said as he sped around a semi.

"I know," Kevin said.

"I never asked before, but did anything stick out in the seaplane pictures?" I asked. "You sent them to the lab, right?"

"Tatum's seaplane is registered in Louisiana," Chase said. "And the word, Lacosta is painted in yellow on the tail."

"Why Lacosta?" Kevin asked.

The gas station appeared, and silence followed. Chase slowed the cruiser as we passed the exit. Everything appeared normal. The very same watermelon truck was parked in front but was empty now.

"Clean up fast," Chase said.

My heart sank for Kevin. He was sitting a few feet behind me, but it felt like we were on different continents. The thought of him holding Rose, her limp body smeared in blood, was too much. I could see the dead driver and the red blood on his white gloves. Tatum's smiling face and teardrop tattoo were clear and real. As we passed the exit, I watched the gas station peel away from the road through the side view mirror.

Chase pushed the pedal to the floor and the cruiser raced over one hundred miles an hour. He shook his head in frustration for the fatal event and reached for another cigar. I finally turned to look at Kevin. He was stone-faced without acknowledgement of anything or anyone around him. The familiar blue eyes I had known my entire life were pressed with sadness. He had become a strange passenger on a mission without the possibility of a happy ending.

* * *

Shortly after crossing the seven-mile bridge, Chase turned the police cruiser off US 1 and passed a green sign that read, Duck Key. He parked in a motel lot next to a line of empty boat trailers backed up against a fence littered with rotten crab trap floats that hung from torn black rope.

"His place is behind the motel on the Gulf side," Chase said. "We have to walk for a little while. Pink stilt house surrounded by mangroves."

He loaded the magazine of his gun and replaced the butt of a cigar with a toothpick. I waited for Kevin's reaction to the gun.

"How many are there?" Kevin asked.

"My guy says five but who knows? That was yesterday."

"What's the plan then?" I asked.

Kevin pulled out both .44 magnums and checked each magazine. He turned to nod at me.

Chase cleared his throat. "We want him brought in alive, Kevin."

"Sure, Chase. Whatever you want."

"My career depends on that. I know you want him dead, just trust me that prison is a far worse punishment than death."

The comment made sense to any sane person. But Kevin was far from sane, and I knew his broken heart would only accept death as an outcome. I nodded approval and Kevin half smiled at the request. You could hear the morning tides close in along both coastlines with a silent empty road behind us. Kevin got out and walked alone in the twilight. His demeanor was clearly different now. I looked at Chase for a reaction, but his attention was on our periphery and not Kevin.

"Guys," I said. "Shouldn't we talk about—"

"Over there, Chase," Kevin said. "I see someone on the roof."

Kevin pointed to the roof of an abandoned house adjacent to the parking lot we were walking through. Chase stopped to look in that direction. I noticed a small figure dressed in black, facing the Atlantic Ocean.

"He's packing something, Chase," Kevin said. "Shotgun looks bigger than he does."

"I don't need kids involved here," Chase said. "Tatum always puts them on the payroll before the fifth grade. He's notorious for using his children for protection."

"Asshole," Kevin said. "Not surprising though."

Chase made a hand gesture to follow him along the rear wall of the house. We passed a pile of crab traps toward thick mangroves. I kept my eyes on the rooftop gunman until we were out of sight inside the natural cover of mangled greens and browns.

"You two know we can't just walk up to the front door, right?" Chase said. "These guys don't small talk."

"So, what are we doing here?" Kevin asked. "I didn't sign up for a stake-out."

"There should only be a couple of them," Chase said. "Three guys tops and a few decoy kids. And if Tatum's there, he'll think Chief Diggs sent me. He shouldn't remember either one of you from the gas station."

I watched the gunman on the roof. He stood as still as a blue heron at low tide. Gun pointed to the early morning sky. Eyes on autopilot, he scanned from one end of the house to the coastline and back again.

"Let me go alone," Kevin said. "I can act like a local fisherman. Hell, maybe a client told me about them? Maybe I'm in need of heroin? You know, business sucks . . . the wife is driving me crazy."

Kevin spoke in a matter-of-fact voice, one that I knew well. His eyes were wide open. My heart was jumping out of my chest at the thought of his request. Chase narrowed his eyes and looked at the gunman on the roof. He nodded slowly and cleared his throat.

"You want to be a hero?" Chase asked. "My guy says this house has the arsenal of a third world country. He watched dealers come and go for days. Million-dollar, center console boats, forty feet long with four outboards dropped anchor ten yards from here . . . yesterday, guys wearing rags holding suitcases full of tens of thousands, garbage bags of cocaine. Locals know to ignore random gunshots at all hours of the night."

"Local cops ignore it?" I asked.

"Money is power. They could blow up a tanker out here and nobody would say a word."

"I'm going up there," Kevin said. "Thanks for the pep talk."

"Here we go," I said. "Are you ready to die too, Kevin?"

Kevin ignored my plea and began to walk away from our cover, through a narrow patch of mangroves. He leaned down and stepped over roots the same way he did as a kid. I never could keep up with him through mangroves. He moved through any kind of foliage with relative ease.

"Not a good idea," Chase said.

Kevin turned and made eye contact with me. His jaw tight and eyes alive and blue as the backdrop of Atlantic Ocean. I knew this was the beginning of the end for our normal life together. He was an emotional wreck and there was no way to stop him.

"What do we do?"

"Cover his ass. Follow me."

Chase pulled a small revolver from his shorts pocket and handed it to me. I opened the chamber to check for bullets. It was loaded and I placed it against my belt with the cool metal pressing hard on the small of my back and followed Chase through the perimeter of the parking lot.

A younger couple walked out of a motel room and passed without suspicion. They were smiling and holding hands. Chase stopped and waited for them to climb inside a full-size pickup truck before he went any farther.

"We need to be discreet about how we do this, Butch. There's a small opening on the other side of this motel that will get us close enough to see the front door. Assuming Kevin will try that entrance."

"How would I know? Makes the most sense, I guess."

"There, you see that path over there?"

Chase pointed at a tiki bar patio below a crop of wild banana trees where a thin patch of grass ran between the buildings.

"I see it. You first."

Chase nodded and I followed him until the road and motel disappeared behind us. We were on the opposite side of the house now. A canopy of palm trees formed above us. The first rays of sunlight showed on the distant waterline.

I stopped at the edge of our cover and watched Chase crawl to the shoreline, every movement methodical until he froze and pointed up at the roof about fifteen yards away. The stilt house was pink and sand gray with a tin roof that lit up in the morning sunlight. Two seaplanes floated parallel to each other at the end of a long pier behind the house.

Kevin finally appeared at the base of the wooden staircase that led up to an oak brown door and marble lion statue. He turned to scan the perimeter until his eyes met mine in the shade. I motioned for him to rejoin us, but he nodded and began to walk up.

I noticed two men walk out on the rear second story balcony. Chase could see them too from his vantage point, but Kevin could not from the front door. The men were talking in broken Spanish and laughing about something.

"Are those shotguns?" Chase asked. "Think they're both strapped with shotguns. Maybe we should have gone up there with him."

"Or called the Miami PD for backup. We need to get up there. Maybe we should've waited."

"Talk to your brother. Tatum's guys may be cool with us at first. At least until we blow our cover."

Chase stood up and began to walk toward the front stairs. I watched two men on the balcony. Their conversation seemed heated now. The gunman on the roof leaned over a downspout and joined in with a high-pitched voice. I turned to follow Chase up the staircase but stopped when one of them made eye contact with me.

"Hold on a minute. One of them is watching us."

"Relax and just follow my lead, Butch."

One of the men leaned over the balcony and watched us. He nodded and lowered his shotgun. I froze and waited for him to walk down the rear staircase. A brown, wind-burned face with black eyes stood eye level with me in ten seconds.

"Detective Anderson," Chase said. "He walked past me and held up his badge. "We need a word with Tatum Jones."

"Hold up, you want to speak with Tone?" he asked with a wide smile. "You're Diggs's boy, right? Crazy gringo from Atlanta, no?"

The other man closed in behind him. They looked like twins, wearing yellow flip-flops, torn brown cargo shorts and Brazilian soccer shirts. Both gripped sawed-off 12-gauge shotguns. Both smelled like weed and red snapper.

"Tone is coming behind you," the other said with a row of gold teeth.

"Who's this, Anderson?" the first one asked.

"My partner, Detective Sands," Chase said. "We're here, off the record."

The one standing uncomfortably close to me gave an approving nod and opened his cell phone. He dialed and put it to his ear. I looked up and noticed the gunman on the roof was watching us. His gun pointed directly at my face. I stared down the barrel and remembered that Kevin was still up there. When I turned to look, he was gone from the front porch.

"Are you coming down?" the first one said into his cell phone. "Diggs sent a few of his boys down. Anderson and Sands want to see you about something."

He listened in silence for almost a full minute. Chase gave me a concerned look and nodded in the direction where Kevin stood minutes before.

"Yes, sir. I understand, sir," he said and closed the cell phone.

"What'd he say?" the other one asked.

He ignored his partner and slid the cell phone inside a shorts pocket and cleared his throat. A hundred scenarios ran through my head. Chase remained calm. I understood that this kind of encounter was probably normal for him. He had acted more nervous when we met with Kevin at Leo's Diner.

"We'll take your guns first," the one with the cell phone said. "All of your guns."

"Wait, I can't give you the—"

"You'll get it back. . . eventually," the first one said. "Tone won't see you strapped."

"I'll help myself then, Anderson."

Chase reluctantly handed over both guns. He motioned for me to hand them the revolver. All power and invincibility disappeared when they turned away with our only chance of survival.

"Now, walk up the steps and go straight inside until you find the kitchen."

"Yeah, the ladies should be making his breakfast," the other one said and looked down at a gold Rolex watch.

Chase stepped around them and walked up the steps. I followed him. We both paused at the front door.

"Remember. . . I'm asking the questions here. Just sit back and listen, gather information, whatever you need to do," Chase said and knocked once with a mounted gold lion's head. "Forget about Kevin as hard as that sounds. It's too late to change our situation. He's in there and they have no idea. We can't change this scenario. Your brother is insane. I should've planned this better. Never should've brought you two down here. This could end up being a fatal mistake. I could lose my job just for giving a known criminal my police issued pistol. Guys get fired for that."

"Forget the guns. Sounds like you've known this guy for years. Thought you've been chasing him?"

"It's classified, Butch," Chase said with eyes focused on the closed door. "You journalists always need to know everything."

I shrugged and waited for Chase to open the unlocked door. He stopped to look around it before entering. I followed him inside. The high-pitched sound of an espresso machine came from the end of the hallway. A strong coffee aroma filled the front foyer. We walked through a winding hallway and passed a water fountain toward a white tiled room crowded with hanging gun racks. Samurai swords were everywhere on the far wall and multiple flat screen televisions showed everything from weather to horse racing. A large painting of the New York City skyline hung over the fireplace mantle above a big emerald Buddha, and a stack of mangled driftwood was stacked inside the fireplace on an iron grate. The dark and wonderfully detailed oil painting distracted me from the immediate threat around us. Chase kept walking around the corner of the room toward the kitchen.

"Surprise, surprise!" a jovial voice said from the kitchen. "What's it been, Anderson, four months at least. It was that South Beach strip club, right?"

I caught up with Chase in the kitchen. Three women in bright pink bikinis stopped cooking to stare at me. They were big boned with long dark hair extensions and silver polished fingernails. Key Lime pies covered a white marble kitchen island.

"Where's Chief Diggs?" Tatum Jones asked. "Did he send you over here?"

I made eye contact with Tatum Jones and froze. Chase recognized this and pulled out a chair from the round table. The sound of wood against tile interrupted the uncomfortable silence. Chase motioned for me to sit down and lit a cigarette.

"Have a seat, Butch," Chase said.

"Yes . . . please, make yourself comfortable, Butch," Tatum said. "You new to this beat?"

"Yeah, showing this rookie the ropes," Chase said and sat down next to Tatum Jones. "Two weeks on the job and he still acts like every day is his first."

"Imagine that," Tatum said with a half-smile. "Have we met before? You have a familiar face."

"Doesn't he look like a C student, frat boy?" Chase said and exhaled. "Chief Diggs sees something there . . . always thought I'd roll solo down here."

Tatum looked back at the three bikini clad women and made a subtle gesture. They all nodded and walked out of the kitchen down another hallway. He raised both eyebrows at us and waited in silence until a door opened and shut.

"Now, Chase, Diggs knows I'm awful tight this week. You can't expect me to supply you and your friend, can you?" Tatum asked and let out a comical, rumbling laugh. "Sure, Tone, he told me about it. It's just that, we have a meeting tonight with Jose's crew. Kind of need product first."

Tatum leaned forward, elbows to table, and sighed. He looked at me with brown, saucer eyes without turning his head. Chase froze at the sight of something behind my chair. I ignored his reaction and stared directly at Tatum until he looked away at Chase.

"You are just in time for some Egyptian Gold blend," Tatum said. "College kids buying up our supply daily."

"What about some coffee, Tatum?" Chase asked. "We've been awake all night."

"Like your women," Tatum said and snapped his fingers. "Bold over ice."

"Absolutely," Chase said. "You want an iced coffee, partner?"

I nodded yes and fought the temptation to turn around to see what Chase saw behind me. Kevin was smarter than just walking out of a closet with guns blazing. Chase looked at something behind me. One of the bikini cooks walked in and stopped at our table. Her head was down, focused on the 12-gauge pistol grip sawed off shotgun in her small left hand. The gun ran along her bare leg and stopped at her kneecap. She waited in silence. Tatum pointed at Chase.

"My man needs an iced coffee, black," Tatum said. "Get Butch the same thing. He looks more like a cream and sugar guy though. That right, Butch?"

"Sure."

She smiled at me, and I tried my best not to look at her curves, barely covered by the pencil thin bikini. I needed to lighten the mood and keep Tatum's attention at the table.

"Keep pouring sugar until the spoon stands up," I said.

"Okay sweetheart," she said and set the shotgun on the kitchen counter, within arm's reach.

Chase and Tatum were fixated on her. She wasn't one of the initial three women. She was out of place here. Model material. I stayed focused on the shotgun. This moment was even more uncomfortable than the first introduction. I took the opportunity to turn around and scan the room. Kevin was nowhere in sight. The adrenaline rush remained with the thought of him shooting Tatum Jones, closet doors slamming open with guns blazing. It felt like I could die, at any time.

"It's not like Diggs to send you unannounced, Anderson," Tatum said. "We flew to Bimini to meet a supplier last week. He never mentioned a hit on Jose."

Chase ashed his cigarette in a gray clamshell and continued to watch the woman in the kitchen make his coffee. She was meticulous with the glass, French press. He finally looked away from her to make eye contact with Tatum.

"He doesn't know we're here," Chase said. "Jose is small time compared to this Mayor scandal you've created."

"Then why are you here? Why bring a rookie, unannounced into my home? Most police officers go years without ever seeing my face let alone my kitchen. Guns too?"

"Rookie is here by mistake. Diggs wasn't supposed to schedule our ride-along until next week."

Chase continued to focus on Tatum. He leaned back in his chair as she placed a cup of iced black coffee on a mint green saucer in front of him. The ceramic mug was the same yellow as her bikini. She set my iced coffee in front of me. It was loaded with cream and sugar. I nodded thanks.

"I'm really here to discuss the gas station," Chase said. "Routine business decision."

Tatum leaned forward, gold rings on all eight fingers dragging across the table. He smiled at the woman and snapped his fingers. She quickly pulled one of the pies from the counter and set it down in front of her master.

"You eat Key Lime pie, Butch?" Tatum asked.

"Sure."

"Of course, you do. Who doesn't love it?"

"I love Key Lime pie," Chase said chain smoking now. Tatum sat back and took a bite of the pie. He smiled at the taste and nodded approval. I was starving and wanted pie. Chase cleared his throat and leaned back in his chair.

"I'd love a—"

"People say one of Florida's first millionaires, William Curry, had a cook named, Aunt Sally, who created it. Say she concocted it from

Key limes in the eighteen hundreds or some shit. So, I always wonder about the poor bastards in the seventeen hundreds who lived without it."

Tatum took another bite of pie and looked over at Chase. The jovial mood was gone. Something bothered him and it showed.

"Know what it's like to live without something you love, Anderson?" Tatum asked and leaned back. "Politicians love to take shit from me. Happens every day in my city."

Chase scooped some pie with his index finger and ate it. Tatum smirked at the act and shook his head. He looked over at the shotgun on the counter and the smirk disappeared.

"Funny what happens when you combine lime juice, sweetened condensed milk, and egg yolks," Tatum said. "Pie cooks itself without any heat."

There was a long silence at the table. I stared at the round Key Lime pie between the three of us. Walking in here was a fatal mistake. I knew it and Chase knew it too. Tatum's persona had changed from cordial host to drive-by killer within minutes after tasting the pie.

"I don't waste time, especially when she's on the itinerary," Tatum said as he turned his attention back to Chase. "Diggs never sends surprises down here, maybe in Miami, but never in the Keys. I don't buy that he's a rookie and I've been wondering about your bearded friend this whole time. Will he or won't he come out from the poolroom? Does he have the balls to shoot at me in my house? Because, for some reason, your third ingredient must be suicidal or crazy. . . maybe both."

I was stunned and unable to move from my seat. Chase remained calm as usual. But I had no idea that Tatum knew about Kevin. This moment would lead to chaos.

"Bullshit," Chase said.

Tatum reached for the green saucer and pulled it toward him. He let out a bellowing laugh and took a sip of the coffee. I was ready to run.

"You still the craziest white cop I've ever known. Be a shame to erase you and your partner over some punk ass lobbyist at a gas station."

His lack of compassion for anyone else hurt or killed at the gas station was expected. If Kevin were within earshot, gunshots would fire any second. I looked away from Tatum and scanned the kitchen. Blue and green tile covered the wall behind the stainless-steel sink. Long wooden tribal faces were mounted on both walls. I studied the one with red eyes and wide brown nose over buckteeth and a bushy goatee, anything to distract my true feelings. Time began to crawl and the alligator clock above the stove seemed to skip every other second. My stomach growled for pie.

"It wasn't just a lobbyist," Chase said pulling the green saucer back toward him. "You shot up the entire gas station."

"So?"

"You also killed—"

Gunshots rang out from the hallway. A woman screamed and the sound of a body slamming against a wall followed. Chase sprang to his feet, throwing the cup of coffee at Tatum. I turned away and ran down the hallway without caution or care. Instinct set in, I was an animal looking for cover.

"Butch! Get out now!" Chase yelled before Tatum tackled him. "The other way."

I turned to see Tatum lunging toward the sawed off 12 gauge on the kitchen counter. Chase turned away from him and ran toward the front door.

"Are you insane, Kevin?" Chase yelled. "This is suicide!"

"Toy cops don't faze me. Why don't you ask Black Bart the same question?" Tatum asked with a relaxed pose. "You all cooked yourselves."

He cocked the assault weapon and pointed it directly at me.

I scanned the room but still no sign of Kevin.

"Think you can walk into my house, especially on Saturday with a fresh pot brewing? Homemade pies in the kitchen."

Chase focused like a laser on Tatum. He stared him down the way he would a cleanup hitter in the bottom of the ninth, two outs, bases loaded. I knew now that his greatest strength was calmness during crisis. Nothing excited him.

"Calm down, Tone. We're leaving in one minute. We're walking out the front door . . . all three of us . . . that's it."

I followed suit and raised both hands. There was still no sign of Kevin. The women stayed in the back room.

"Fools get smoked on a daily basis," Tatum said. "You should know by now, Anderson. I only deal with Diggs. Not you . . . and not your damn puppets."

"You killed —"

"You talking again, rookie? Nobody asked you a damned thing," Tatum said, looking at Chase as he spoke. "Control your boy before his ass is filled with elephant slugs."

"Butch . . . shut the hell up!" Chase said then cleared his throat and stepped between us.

"So, what about that politician? He had it coming to him. You just can't evict half a city block of good Cuban people and expect to get away with it. You know what I'm saying?" Tatum smiled, exposing an upper row of gold teeth. "This my town. We're controlling things . . . not some yuppie dude living on South Beach collecting rent. I pay out more in hush money a day than you make in a year. Believe that rookie."

Chase gave me a look to stay quiet. He leaned over to look through the window at the men on the dock. Both seaplanes were still tied off to the dock.

"Are you listening, Anderson?" Tatum asked and rubbed the thin facial hair on his chin. "Diggs knew what was going down even before it happened. Doesn't he let you know these things?" He covered his mouth and laughed. "Shit, did I just say that?"

"You're a dead man, Tone," Chase said.

"Going against me is suicide, Anderson," Tatum said with a golden smile. "Writing your death certificate."

Chase remained calm and nodded toward the front door. I began to walk toward it. It was amazing we were still alive.

"Take your ass out. My guys should be up here in about five seconds. I like you too much to kill you, Anderson. Leave that up to them. Saving my energy for pie."

The sound of feet running up the front stairway came within seconds. I looked at Chase and then turned away in anticipation before the front door slammed open.

"Run, Anderson!" Tatum said and folded his arms.

"It's over, Tone—"

POP POP . . . POP POP POP!

Gunfire erupted as the front door slammed open. I turned and sprinted down the hallway and sprinted out to the back porch. Chase brushed by me and jumped off the balcony without hesitation. He caught a thin branch from a pine tree and broke the two-story fall. I jumped for the same branch and missed but the thick trunk slowed my fall, and I rolled forward in the sand and landed below the shade of mangroves.

"Let's go, Butch!" Chase said and motioned for me to follow him toward the dock. "Kevin's waiting."

Just then the propellers from one of the Otter Seaplanes began to spin. I noticed Kevin in the cockpit. He was frantically waving us over. I tripped on a raised deck board and fell forward against the last piling. Chase stood on the long float and pulled me over. I followed him inside with the sound of gunfire closing in behind us.

I crawled in the small backseat and leaned down. Kevin adjusted his headset and handed Chase a gun. The seaplane engine roared and drowned out the screams and gunshots coming for us. Chase leaned out the window and fired five consecutive shots as Kevin pulled a one-eighty in front of the cover of mangroves and accelerated away from the dock. I buckled my seat belt and held on to the back of the seat for balance. Minutes later the mangroves were gone, and the blue water fell away from us.

The Gulf of Mexico moved a hundred feet below in a shaken blur. Kevin pulled back until we reached an altitude of about three hundred feet and flew over the seven-mile bridge. I slapped Kevin's shoulder and closed my eyes, grateful to be alive.

Chapter Nine

Saltwater smacked the nose of our seaplane. The force toppled us over and drove the left wing underwater. My seatbelt held me down as the fuselage went vertical. I reached over to pull Kevin back. He sat motionless in the front seat. Chase was frantic about his seatbelt until it finally released. He immediately clicked Kevin free just as warm saltwater filled the cockpit. Together, we pulled Kevin out through the shattered front windshield. Adrenaline and fear masked the struggle to keep him above water. Chase turned Kevin over on his back and held his bearded chin up. The plane bobbed halfway underwater as we swam toward Cayo Costa Island.

"Just look at the sand, Butch," Chase said. "Don't even think about what we are doing right now. Just watch the sand and kick your ass off."

"Okay. Is he breathing?"

"Watch the sand."

Saltwater filled my nose and throat, and the afternoon sunlight warmed the top of my head and shoulders. I focused on kicking my legs and watched the white line of sand move with the choppy surf and hoped Kevin was alive. There was no way to tell. He was limp and motionless.

I sensed something below us just as my lower torso was bumped. Another one came within seconds and a dark figure swam in a spiral motion below us. A surface splash followed, and Chase reached behind him and let go of Kevin's chin. I grabbed his wet beard and kept his mouth and nose above the water.

"Are those sharks?" I asked. "Why'd you let go?"

"They're smaller than sharks and they're brown," Chase said. "Just watch the beach and keep him up. I'll handle this. Kick your ass off, Butch!"

A school of long, brown fish appeared just beneath my feet as a frenzy ensued. Water smacked my face and limited all visibility. I stayed focused on Kevin and kept kicking.

"They're cobia, Butch! But why in the hell are cobia this close to us? Where are the hammerheads?"

I noticed a pool of blood forming around Kevin's right ear and realized he injured it during the crash. The splashing finally stopped, and I could see Chase a few yards back. He held his .44 at an angle and pointed at the school of cobia below us.

"It's Kevin. He's bleeding from his ear. Looks cut or something," I said.

"The beach . . . just kick toward the beach."

Just then the school of cobia forced Chase underwater. I wanted to help but stayed focused on the beach and keeping Kevin from drowning. Chase resurfaced and fired three rounds down at the school. He splashed and kicked until he was parallel with us to the beach. I finally felt sand on my feet and was relieved to have support. Together, we pulled Kevin toward the scorching sand. The frenzy ensued a few yards behind us.

We dragged Kevin through the hot white sand until we reached the shade of a tan gumbo-limbo tree. Chase lifted his chin and listened for breathing. He clasped both hands and did ten quick chest compressions before filling his lungs with two quick breaths of air. I wanted to help but knew that timing was everything.

"Wake up, Kevin!" Chase said. "Come on Kev."

I turned away from another attempt and watched the distant seaplane bob a few more times before going completely underwater. The ripple around the tail wing spread out into the school of cobia still frantically looking for blood on the surface. The Pedro Island lighthouse filled in the seascape. The welcoming sight reminded me of Hailey Thomas.

"He's breathing, Butch."

Kevin rolled to one side and began coughing up saltwater uncontrollably. His bloodshot eyes grew wide with the sight of Chase Anderson leaning over him with a big smile.

* * *

We sat facing one another with backs against two pine tree trunks. The pine needles blanketed the surrounding area and their smell had calmed my nerves just enough to rest. Kevin had not said a word for a long time and Chase kept looking at his waterlogged guns. I kept watch on the moving current that ran over the top of where the seaplane sank in the pass, hoping for a random fishing boat to appear and take us home. Hammerheads and tarpon had a new playground eighty feet down with a yard full of broken jigs.

"What happened up there, Kevin?" Chase said. "I thought you had it."

"I tried to land but lost control in that wind. Thank you for what you did for me."

"You saved us down there; I should be thanking you. Have you ever flown a seaplane before?"

I caught Kevin's eye contact and smiled. Our father used to take us up when we were younger. He had a charter friend who ran little neck clams to Miami for a wealthy client. Kevin always watched him fly while I watched the trailing landscape below us. His memory was practically photographic.

"First time without a pilot sitting next to me."

"Bullshit. You were a pro up there."

"Our dad used to take us up with a family friend," I said. "Kevin must have learned on the fly, literally."

"I'll take the fly-rod every time over flying," Kevin said with a smile.

We laughed in unison and for a moment all was forgotten. For now, we were three guys sitting around after a long day on the water. I missed that, Kevin. It was good to know his soul was still alive.

"So, where the hell are we now?" Chase asked.

"Cayo Costa Island," Kevin said.

Chase made eye contact with me and tilted his head. I shrugged and waited for it. He finally set the guns down on the pine needles and stood up. The Pedro Island lighthouse was small on the distant beach behind him.

"The same Cayo Costa, Butch?" Chase pointed behind him.

"Yeah, same one."

Kevin had a confused look. He cleared his throat and stood up next to Chase. I stayed seated. They both looked at me with tired eyes. Their clothes were wet rags.

"So where is it?"

"Where's what?" Kevin asked. "What's he asking you?"

"The money," Chase said. "Does it really exist?"

"Yes."

"Money from what?"

Chase stepped forward and had the same look from our first meeting at his Miami PD office. He knew I was lying then. But now, we were together on something bigger than both of us. He just saved my brother's life. He risked everything by going after Tatum Jones without the Miami PD. I could finally trust him.

"Why does it matter?"

"We need resources right now. Without Miami PD, I got nothing. We need money to chase Tatum Jones. And we'll need an arsenal to find him."

Kevin cleared his throat. He pulled at his rugged beard, and I knew the tough questions were coming.

"Kevin, before you ask, let me explain a few things. There is more to this than money."

"But you gave it back to the guy's son in Gainesville. Stevie, the baseball player, right? That's what you told me, Hailey, even mom."

I stood to face them both. The buried money was secret for over a month now. My time stranded on that Caribbean Island changed how I treated people. Whether or not I could trust anyone. Even those I loved most. Watching a stranger die the way Vic Turner died was difficult. But it taught me a valuable lesson, too, about life and what matters most.

"I kept a promise to a dying man . . . someone who saved my life. He wanted me to have half of it and do something great. I was prepared to leave it buried here for thirty years if nothing came up. I thought I could keep it a secret until the time was right to dig it up and live the rest of my life with Hailey . . . worry free."

"We need it," Chase said. "Even some of it will make or break this whole thing."

I made eye contact with Kevin and could see the urgency in him. His breathing had slowed but his tense shoulders and raised eyebrows reminded me of his need to keep moving until Tatum Jones was dead.

"I know. Just stay put and give me some time to find the box. Please respect that."

"Take as much time as you need. We'll figure out a way off this island. Our cell phones are waterlogged and worthless now."

Chasing Palms

* * *

A local fishing guide found us an hour after I handed Chase and Kevin a hundred thousand each. I kept a hundred thousand, too. They both reacted with a similar, surprised look. The topic of money faded fast when Kevin spotted a familiar boat drifting close to the beach.

Kevin recognized the boat and guide from a fishing tournament they competed in months earlier and caught his attention just after his first toss of a cast-net along the shallow point of the island. He picked us up and offered to drop us at Tarpon Marina. He and Kevin talked shop for the short trip across the pass while I sat in the lone fighting chair and watched the wake from the two 150 horsepower outboards off the stern of *Kelly*, a thirty-foot yellow center console.

Chase smoked a cigarette he had bummed from the guide and made random eye contact with a smug look across his now sunburnt face. I think he was still in disarray over the buried money. Maybe he believed my lies during his initial interrogation.

Kevin helped dock *Kelly* near the Tarpon Marina fuel tanks. After Chase bummed another cigarette. He nodded thanks to our savior and stepped up on the worn wooden dock. He walked fast toward the marina without saying a word to Kevin or me.

"I really appreciate your help," I said to the guide.

"No problem. Kevin would've done the same for me," the guide said. "How'd you guys end up stranded anyway?"

I looked at Kevin, who gestured that I follow Chase. The question was such a loaded one that it was better left unanswered. I turned my attention to Chase who was walking past the marina now.

"Meet me at the house, Kevin," I said. "Couple hours."

"Sure, see you in a few."

I caught up with Chase in the front parking lot. Evening was setting in and yellow streetlamps began to blink on. He took one final drag from the cigarette and tossed it on the cracked concrete.

"How much is still buried over there?" Chase asked. "Three hundred thousand isn't a million."

"Why would I say that? I just handed you a hundred thousand dollars. Why are you still questioning me about the money?"

Chase turned to face the empty street behind him. His shorts pockets were bulging with stacks of money bound by rubber bands. He nervously held one of the stacks of money with one hand and rubbed his forehead with the other, the way you would for a migraine. Both guns were held by a leather belt and stuck out from the small of his back.

"Look, you and Kevin could disappear tonight, no problem. But we met with Tone . . . without my boss, Chief Diggs. Hell, we had a shootout with him, crashed his seaplane and probably killed a few of his top guys."

"I know I was there. When did this—"

"Follow me inside for a minute," Chase said. "I need another cigarette in the worst way."

He turned back around to face me. The overconfident, cocky pitcher had a new look of fear in his narrow blue eyes. This was the first time I felt like he needed us more than we needed him.

I followed him inside the marina office and waited in silence. He bought everything they had, twelve cartons of cigarettes. The clerk's eyes widened when he accidentally pulled out a hundred-dollar bill from his gangster roll.

He stopped just outside to open a box and lit one with a pack of matches he grabbed off the counter. His smoking hand shook slightly but became steady after the third drag.

"Grace never let me smoke in the apartment we shared," Chase said. "Spent most conversations talking to her through a cracked sliding glass door. We lived on the third floor in a small harbor complex."

He turned and pointed at the yachts and center consoles that crowded Tarpon Marina. A smile showed and the nervousness seemed to fade with the memory.

"We could never agree on a boat either. Always thought we'd make enough to own something, eventually, once we paid off Florida State Law School for her. She thought the thirty-foot sailboats were just big enough for us. I always wanted a forty-foot center console with four three-fifties. You know, something to get me thirty miles out in the deeper parts of the Gulfstream."

I stared at my dreamboat on stilts ten yards from where Chase was standing now. His memory sparked my own need for something to get me thirty miles out in a hurry. I smiled at the thought of Hailey ever agreeing to buy something that expensive when we could own a smaller sailboat our future family could enjoy.

"Let's think this through, Butch. Because like it or not, we're all in now. Tatum Jones is more than likely meeting with the Chief today if not tomorrow. Wish I could be there to see the look on Chief's face when he finds out I wasn't patrolling South Beach on foot this morning."

I ignored whatever Chase said next and watched the marina. Kevin stood on a distant dock talking to the same guide that found us stranded. He was facing the dry storage building but the sulk in both shoulders and limited movement told me his mind was somewhere else.

"Butch? Why aren't you answering?" Chase asked.

"Sorry, what did you say? Just checking on Kevin out there."

Chase turned to look at Kevin who was walking toward the fuel tanks now. Hunger found its way in my thoughts, and I realized that none of us had eaten all day. I looked up at the yellow lights and fought an incredible urge to eat.

"Kevin's fine, Butch. I asked what your plan was for tomorrow. Because I'm leaving for Miami after I find some food. I'm starving. We need to talk about how you and Kevin plan to hide out until I get back tomorrow night."

"Why are you going to Miami?"

"To meet with my guy. He'll know Tatum Jones's next move. Even though I'm certain he's flying to New Orleans as we speak."

"Let's head that way now. Why wait until tomorrow? Kevin won't agree to wait."

Chase lit a third cigarette off the tip of the second and leaned in closer to make eye contact. He exhaled out the side of his mouth and smiled. His narrow eyes widened some as if he seemed to wonder how I came to that kind of conclusion without asking him his opinion first.

"We need more guns."

I nodded and stepped back away from his stare. He was too much at times. A hundred thousand dollars in cash made it worse. He had acted somewhat invincible ever since I handed him the money.

"Right. Go get the guns. Find out where he's going. I'll keep Kevin at bay until tomorrow night. Just don't make it longer than that."

"Good. Meet me right here, eleven o'clock tomorrow night."

"Okay. How will we communicate until then?"

"We won't. The Miami PD has ears everywhere."

Chase turned away and walked beneath the flickering yellow lights toward the winding street. No cars had passed the marina since we started talking. Sagging shorts and a filthy shirt gave him some semblance of a local.

Chapter Ten

I thought of the familiar silhouette of Captain Dan, bulging stomach and bushy gray beard, leaned forward against the railing of a grand lanai on the North end of Pedro Island that faced the mouth of Stump Pass, an eighty-foot-deep utopian fishery he knew better than anyone. He used to take my father tarpon fishing. I remember those cool April mornings from my youth when Kevin and I helped our father, James, outfit his fishing gear hours before sunrise. We always begged him to go but our mother never let us. She was too afraid of the hammerheads that ruined it for most fishermen. She feared for our safety more than any hooked hundred-pound tarpon. I still hate hammerhead sharks for both reasons.

I walked along the evening-cooled sand toward Captain Dan's beach house. The shoreline had shifted some over the past few years. Shallow sandbars fought daily with the moving currents that pushed the sandy floor out toward the wide expanses of the Gulf of Mexico. Large pieces of driftwood clung to the curve in the beach, and small schools of pinfish swam inside waves that rolled and crashed before my bare feet.

Captain Dan owned the large gray house on the point. It had a tin roof and rested high on stilts twenty yards back from the waterline. I walked past the full green leaves and dangling clusters of sea grapes then stopped at the base of wooden steps that lead up toward the entrance of the lanai. When he finally noticed me there a boyish grin ran across his face.

"Butch, where in the hell did you come from?"

"Be right up," I said.

He looked over the iron railing at me with hands on hips. I knew what he was thinking from the peculiar look on his face. Ever since our dad died, he acted like a father to Kevin and me.

"You look terrible, Butch. Shouldn't you be with what's his name again? Chase Anderson or something."

"I'll be right there," I said, ignoring the question.

I walked up splintered steps to face him. He reached out to shake my hand and pulled me in for an expected bear hug. Fishing gear was scattered on the table.

"Damn, I'm glad you're still here. Your mother called three times this week asking about you boys. Where's Kevin?"

"He's out in the pass," I said without really knowing.

"Figures. Have a seat. I'll have Lana make us some coffee. You hungry?"

"Thanks. I'm good with just coffee."

His brown eyes were folded inside crows' feet wrinkles below unkempt gray eyebrows. He looked tired and I knew the sun and wind had taken a toll on him today, the same as every day. He only missed being out on the water if the weather was life threatening. I remember my father always quoting him as saying, "the tarpon never take a day off in April or May."

He finally let go and sat down at the same table filled with fishing gear. He picked up a yellow coffee mug and took a sip. I noticed a blue canvas fishing hat with several tarpon flies hooked along both sides. There was the familiar fly-tie vice clamped to the side of the table clasping a number four circle hook. I found a seat across from him.

"I had a late night down at Marker 17. Been recovering all day. You're the last person I expected to see walking up from the beach. You look like you slept in the sand last night."

"It was a car, actually."

I rubbed the sleep from my eyes and scanned the distant waterline. Pelicans glided by us toward the beach.

"I know about Rose, Butch. Is Kevin okay?"

A petite woman walked out wearing a green apron. She held a round tray of coffee with a plate of butter and toast. I took the opportunity to reach for an empty ceramic mug and waited for her to pour my coffee. Captain Dan sat back in his chair with a suggestive look.

"No. Kevin's not okay. He's desperate for help. That's why I'm here now."

"Isn't the Miami PD on it? Vince talked about that same detective meeting with you and Kevin at Marker 17 the other night. Said he was kind of cocky and outspoken. Thought he was a baseball player or something at one time. Said he pitched for a minor league baseball team down in Fort Lauderdale about four years ago."

"That's Chase Anderson. He's been tracking Rose's killer for years but hasn't landed him. His Chief is in bed with the same guy."

"Who's the guy?" he asked, leaning forward.

"Tatum Jones. He shot up the same gas station we stopped at on our way down to meet with Miami PD. His target was a young politician with something to prove. Rose was just an innocent victim."

"Beyond comprehension to me."

"Kevin is a different person now."

"Were you at least able to clear your name?"

"I'm kind of working on that now."

"What can I do, Butch?"

I contemplated my answer and took a moment to sit back and look up at the towering Florida pine trees that outlined his rectangular property. Green palmettos dotted the gray landscape below them. A full avocado tree stood out atop a small patch of Bermuda grass along the far corner. Its smooth branches reached up toward the blue tint of twilight and dark narrow fruit hung as still as ornaments on the Christmas trees of my youth. There was no star just a cluster of mangled greens and browns that swayed in the cool gulf winds.

"We went after Tatum Jones yesterday morning . . . and it didn't end well. Kevin saved our lives. But now, Tatum knows who we are and will come after us. To put it in the simplest terms, we need to find him before he finds us."

"Can't Chase Anderson help you with that?"

"Tatum Jones is bigger than Miami PD. He has Chief Diggs in his pocket. I just know we need help, and you can help us. We think Tatum is headed for New Orleans, probably with enough heroin to land him thirty years in prison."

I stood up from the comfortable setting and excellent robust coffee to look out at the dark pass. Kevin could be out there right now, alone in his own darkness.

"We didn't ask for this. It just happened. And now, if I don't stay ahead of it . . . Kevin will do something life changing. Chase Anderson is really my only chance of keeping Kevin out of prison for the rest of his life. But I have a feeling Chase is as desperate as Kevin for very similar reasons."

"I've heard enough to help you, Butch," Captain Dan said. "When do you need to go?"

"Tomorrow night. Chase is meeting us at Tarpon Marina tomorrow at eleven, after he returns from Miami. He's meeting with one of his inside guys tomorrow to confirm that Tatum Jones is actually going to New Orleans."

Captain Dan stood up next to me and faced the same dark water. He crossed thick forearms and smiled a familiar smile. We shared silence and the volume turned down in my mind.

"Come on inside for a minute," Captain Dan said.

He walked in front of me and held the double doors open to let me pass him toward a large open room with a pitched ceiling. A driftwood fire burned in the stone fireplace with blue and purple flames that crackled and turned over. A knot in the biggest piece of wood burst with the heat, sending glowing dots of fire against the iron fence and down onto the hardwood floor.

"I'll need to call Vince to confirm my flight schedule this week," Captain Dan said. "I'm available as long as you need me."

"I truly appreciate it—"

"Don't mention it. James would've done the same for one of my boys, I'm sure of it."

I stood and waited in the great room, absorbing the heat and studied an oil painting of the Pedro Island lighthouse that hung just above a long wooden mantel. The wonderful oil rendition had been painted well with an orange sky, mangrove green background and moving turquoise waterline between Pedro Island and neighboring Cayo Costa Island; the lamp warming just before sunset, below a row of brown pelicans gliding over it toward the concrete pilings of long-ago railroad tracks and the speckled narrows of tall Florida pines.

* * *

The quiet island streets came alive with seagulls and my morning slumber began to fade. I hurried down back streets to avoid seeing anyone who would know me. It's hard to hide from the people you write about, especially when you are a journalist.

I finally reached the long, shell-filled driveway that wound around swaying coconut palms. Kevin's yellow truck was parked in the side yard. I found a handwritten note from Dudas on the unlocked front door and hurried inside to fill a backpack with clothes for the trip to New Orleans.

To my surprise, Kevin lay sprawled out on the couch with the television still on. Empty beer bottles covered the kitchen countertop, and a pizza box sat open on the floor next to the couch. Several fly-ties had been spread across his desk, green and blue and silver. I remembered how Kevin would always tie them to sober up. A plane streamer hook had been left in the vice, and a tidal chart was flat atop the desk with empty beer bottles on each corner.

"Get up, Kev."

Kevin surprisingly sprung up and stood to face me. Long hair covered his red eyes. He took in a few breaths, and I waited for him to get his bearings.

"What time is it, Butch?"

"Almost eight."

He walked over to the small kitchen and pulled a tin coffee can down from an open cabinet. Sunlight crept through closed blinds behind me and seemed to bother his adjusting eyes.

"How long have you been here?" he said. "Did you come home last night?"

"I stayed at Captain Dan's."

I had his full attention as the coffee maker began to percolate. He and Captain Dan had developed a close relationship since our father died years ago. The statement must have caught him off guard.

"Why'd you go there? Does he know about Rose?"

"Yes, he wants to help us."

Kevin slammed a ceramic mug on the kitchen countertop and leaned over with a sullen expression. I knew he was instantly concerned with Captain Dan's safety. He probably never would have involved him for fear of losing someone else important.

"Why? Tatum Jones will kill him either way. If not this week, he'll eventually get to him. He's too easy to find. Knows everybody on the Gulf Coast."

"We need him, Kevin. It just felt right asking."

The coffee maker beeped, and he turned to fill the mug. I watched him drink the steaming coffee the same way our father would every morning I can remember from my youth. No cream, no sugar, thumb around the base, palm against the half-circle with fingers wrapped around the side. He even dropped his bearded chin the same way before every sip.

"I understand why, Butch. And I know he won't accept me telling him not to help. What's the plan?"

Chapter Eleven

The afternoon sun parted gray nimbus clouds away from their hover over Pedro Island. I watched the royal blue wedge of October sky above outreaching pines as Kevin passed the island lighthouse. He insisted we get supplies from Tarpon Marina before we boarded Captain Dan's seaplane tonight.

"When's Chase supposed to call?" Kevin asked. "Why hasn't he called us?"

"No idea. I trust he'll be here tonight."

"This isn't something you just show up for last minute. Chase is going to get us killed."

Kevin hit the tan steering wheel with an open hand and shook his head in frustration. He lit a cigarette, and the smoke calmed him. His casual driving pose appeared as the seat reclined. We sped down a narrow side street along a perfectly cut and sloping golf course fairway as the finality of what I agreed to do settled inside my conscience. My mind trumped fear and worst-case scenario with urgency and reckless abandon. I had the most to lose. Hailey was clueless and still wondering when my flight would land in Mexico. She was there, and would be there waiting, a perfect prize in the end. But there was no good outcome for Kevin or Chase. This was revenge for them. Life would continue regardless for both. Kevin is the real reason for risking everything. Finding my childhood hero again, the way he was, bigger than life with a fishing rod and bucket on a pier at dusk watching Gasparilla Sound. I can still picture him standing on the bow of our fifteen-foot flats boat with a cast-net over his shoulder, watching the water. He was a seven-year-old giant in my four-year-old eyes.

He finally slowed the truck and turned into the back entrance of Tarpon Marina and parked the truck in a vacant employee parking lot. I scanned the empty marina and listened to the rumble of incoming rain.

"I'm going down to see Vince," Kevin said. "You can wait in dry storage if you want. I cannot say how Tatum will react to yesterday."

"Meet back here in what, fifteen minutes?"

"Make it twenty."

He gave me a raised eyebrow look and we were quiet while heavy raindrops began to splatter across the windshield. He reached for the pack of cigarettes and hurried out across the parking lot toward the forklift that sat in its usual place against rusted cleats. Vince, the harbormaster, was nowhere in sight. I watched Kevin turn the corner and remembered last hurricane season and the chaos it caused the island. Damaged sailboats and yachts were everywhere for weeks after the storm.

* * *

The evening rainstorm passed. Captain Dan walked along one of the floats on his white and navy-blue Cessna 185 floatplane. Twilight filled the marina behind him. He bit down on the usual Churchill length cigar inside a wide jaw and gray beard and held the nozzle end of a fifty-foot fuel hose. There was a sudden pause in his action as he scanned the surrounding marina. I turned away to watch the road beyond where the truck was parked behind the dry storage, still no sign of Chase Anderson.

"When's this cop fellow supposed to be here, Butch?"

"No idea. He's driving up from Miami."

Kevin was still inside the marina office. His fifteen minutes always meant an hour, especially before any kind of travel. He was always the most prepared because a guide's preparation is always their client's expectation.

"If Vince asks, let me explain things. Just nod and keep working," Captain Dan said fueling the plane now. "We'll be fine once he gets here."

I trusted that Captain Dan was exactly who we needed for this to work. The real concern was how Chase would react to another person getting involved. I decided to take a walk toward the street alone, and sort things out in my mind.

"I'll be back in a few. Chase should be here soon."

"No problem," Captain Dan said smiling.

I walked past the storefront where Kevin stood facing Vince at the sales counter. They must have been discussing something important because the usually animated Vince was slouched over without his usual wide eyes and flailing arms.

The Cape Dory Explorer was still on blocks behind the marina. Navy-blue hull and twin CAT 3116 diesel engines resting there, waiting for me on cinder blocks, out of their element in the marina mix of sand and exhaust. I walked all forty feet from stern to bow and followed the contour around her nose. The smooth texture from worn fiberglass gave me a sense of security and I realized that most things in life are unpredictable, moving targets. She reminded me of something real, something I could feel, always here waiting for me to outfit. Hailey Thomas is the only woman to ever give me this same feeling. And I knew the coming days would take everything to fall in a perfect line of chance and luck to overcome Tatum Jones, Miami's legendary heroin God who destroyed my brother's reality and devastated a once great baseball player's life.

I stopped thinking and scanned the parking lot. The sun was setting now, and rays of sunlight pushed through tall pines across the quiet street, still no sign of Chase Anderson.

"You're so predictable, Butch," Kevin said. "Just make Vince an offer and get it over with."

I shrugged and stepped away from her as if he caught me doing something illegal. Kevin stood smoking one of Captain Dan's Churchill cigars, hands in the front pocket of fishing overalls. The slightest smile showed behind his unkempt beard. Regardless of how he must have been feeling, he always kept it close to the vest. Kevin was stoic even now, with everything that had happened.

An engine accelerated on the distant road. A black truck sped into the front parking lot and came to a screeching stop behind our truck. Chase jumped out and ran toward us. He was empty handed and sweating profusely.

"Where . . . where's the plane?" Chase asked and took in a deep breath as he waited for the rest to come out. "We need a pilot, right?" Chase acted nervous and constantly looked back at the road as if expecting someone. His nervousness was uncharacteristic. I made eye contact with Kevin, who looked concerned.

"Are you being followed?" Kevin asked.

"Followed? Who's following me . . . I mean us. Been driving straight from Miami."

Kevin pulled a cigarette from his pocket and handed it to Chase, then held up his lighter. I watched the road with anticipation.

"This is deeper than I thought," Chase said. "Chief Diggs is on to us, Butch. I think I was being followed."

"Wait a minute," Kevin said. "Who's following you?"

"No time right now. Where's the plane?" Chase brushed by us toward the marina. "They'll be here soon. I know it."

"Fine. It's back over that way," I said matching his urgency. "But Captain Dan might take a minute or so to finish his preflight."

Chase stopped on a dime and turned to face me. His red eyes were wide with anticipation. The quiet marina moved at a temperate pace behind him. I knew involving Captain Dan was a mistake. Kevin gave me a look that reinforced that feeling.

"Captain Dan?"

"He's like a second father to us," I said. "Only person I could trust for something like this. He'll get us to New Orleans without a hitch."

Chase looked at Kevin, then back at me. The rush of adrenaline hit pause in a moment of shock. I could almost script the next words out of his crooked mouth. Just as the newly lit cigarette began to move in the corner of his mouth, screeching tires sounded from the parking lot.

"These guys won't ask questions," Chase said and pulled a gun from his pants pocket and pulled back the hammer.

I sprinted by him toward the seaplane. Captain Dan noticed me sprinting and jumped inside the cockpit. He left the door open for us. I made it inside the Cessna just as the first gunshots were fired. I hurried in the back seat and watched Kevin running toward us with Chase crouched behind a wooden piling firing round after round at someone standing near the Dory Explorer behind the marina office.

Captain Dan frantically flipped switches as Kevin jumped inside. Chase hurried inside, clutching his gun with both hands.

"Get this bird off the water!" Chase yelled as he reloaded a clip. "Three of them, one has a shotgun. The other two have handguns, I think."

"All right," Captain Dan said and taxied the seaplane away from the fueling tanks. "God, I hope they don't hit the propeller."

Gunfire erupted from the dock behind us. Captain Dan accelerated the seaplane and swung the tail end side to side creating a heavy wake through the marina. Chase kept firing at them. I stayed down and watched the dark waterline through the front window. The seaplane fought against the ebb tide current for a time then started to ascend over the water.

"What happens if they hit the fuel in the wing?" I asked.

"We'll have to chance it," Captain Dan said.

My comfort level returned with the sight of him easing back the controls to change our heading to northwest. The humming sounds combined from the engine and propeller had a soothing effect as I turned to watch the marina shrink and the men fade into darkness.

Chase continued to clutch his gun with both hands even though the gunfight was over. He leaned forward in his seat with tense shoulders. When only dark blue waters filled our horizon, Chase finally seemed to let go and sit back in his seat with the gun resting in his lap. Kevin sat still beside me in the cramped space with arms crossed around his stomach. Both eyes were closed but he was not sleeping.

Soft control lights reminded me of the porch lights Hailey loved to look at on our back lanai. I enjoyed the thought of her warmth and instantly missed her smiling face. Now was the time to relax and close my eyes. So, I focused on the crescent moon that hung like an ornament over the Gulf of Mexico and knew our cover had been blown at Tarpon Marina. Authorities would probably be waiting for us in New Orleans.

I felt guilty for getting Captain Dan involved and wondered what he was thinking. But I knew from experience that he always thought out every possible scenario. He had been preparing for worse case scenarios his entire professional life. We would either find Tatum Jones or he would find us. It was simple to think of in those terms. So, I did, and a calm silence fell over me. The grime and solace of Bourbon Street was a vision that followed Hailey Thomas and the glow of our quiet lanai.

Chapter Twelve

Captain Dan touched down well short of New Orleans, just before midnight, with a flashing fuel light. We landed along a stretch of panhandle coastline. Chase wasted no time and opened the door. I could smell gasoline leaking from the wing.

A cool wind filled our cabin and the propeller wound down after Captain Dan killed the engine. That soothing engine noise was gone, and we sat in silence. I felt an uncomfortable tension in the cabin, and everyone stared at Chase Anderson.

"They were Tatum's guys," Chase said. "Chief Diggs must have tracked me to the apartment."

"You went to your apartment?" Kevin asked. "Of course, they tracked you. Butch said you were meeting with your guy about Tatum's location."

Chase rubbed his temples and cleared his throat. I looked at Kevin in disbelief. We thought Chase was the professional. Captain Dan turned in his seat to look at me with raised eyebrows. He removed the headphones and pulled a flashlight from under his seat and turned it on.

"Regardless, we'll have to spend a day or two repairing that damn wing," Captain Dan said. "There should be a line under one of your seats. Come on. We haven't got all night."

The flashlight lit up the cabin exposing a look of frustration on Kevin's face. A flame flickered as Chase lit a cigarette and stepped outside.

"Here's the damn line, Chase," Captain Dan said. "How far off is the road from here?"

"Hundred yards, maybe two hundred."

"Hang tight, guys," Captain Dan said and flipped the cabin lights on.

Chasing Palms

* * *

The moon offered little light along a dark, continuous beach that stretched for miles in either direction. Chase leaned against a wooden boardwalk, and I could see the orange glow from another cigarette. He watched an access road that paralleled the beach with dimly lit lamp poles every quarter mile. Not one vehicle passed for over an hour. Kevin sat with toes buried in wet sand. He was catching his breath from bearing most of the weight when we pulled the seaplane ashore. It always amazed me how he could find comfort in any environment. Captain Dan stood behind him with a flashlight, reading his flight plan, chewing on a cigar.

I walked through tall sea oats and felt the granular roll of sugar sand against bare feet. Chase continued to watch the empty road as I approached him. His confidence was gone, and the moment felt like a cold sales call. He was nothing like the arrogant detective I first met. Something must have happened in Miami. The trust he had gained was nearly gone.

"I'll get us a car," Chase said and pulled a cell phone from his wet pants pocket. "My cousin, James lives near Destin. He's a Charter Captain."

The cell phone was ruined from saltwater. He shook it a few times before looking at me with crazy eyes. I knew we needed him more than he could ever realize. Kevin's life depended on it.

"Did you see a payphone, Butch?" Chase asked. "What about the street? Notice anyone on the street?"

"What happened in Miami?" I asked. "You're not the same."

"You have no idea what's happening," Chase said. "We tried to assassinate a mega dealer!"

"But you took us—"

"I didn't know Kevin would act like an eight-year-old and hide out in a closet with guns. That was supposed to be a fact-finding mission."

"Why didn't you communicate that on the drive down?"

"Maybe I should've said something, but what's done is done."

"At least Kevin tried to do something about what happened. You just sat back acting like one of Tatum's old friends from high school."

Chase turned and punched a wooden post. He mumbled something and hopped over the railing onto the boardwalk. I had to look up at him from where I stood in the sand.

"You don't know me," Chase said. "I made a commitment to help you and Kevin. You're missing money case brought us together and now, my actions have cost me my job and any chance of ever catching Tatum Jones."

"Catching him? Kevin won't let that happen."

"We'll see about that. Tatum Jones is my ticket for bringing Chief Diggs and everyone else down for what they've been getting away with for years now. If I can't have Grace back . . . then everyone around me will have to deal with the consequences. The Miami PD gives my life purpose. My once in a lifetime love is gone, forever."

There was a long pause. I had become a referee on a deadly chase. The realization stung and clawed at my insides. Kevin lay still against a life vest yards away. I knew he could hear us, but he chose to stay away from this conversation. His opinion did not matter to Chase. He probably wanted to know the ulterior one just presented in a fit of smoke and dim moonlight.

"I'm going to get some sleep while I can," I said and turned away.

"I'm dying too," Chase said.

I nodded without turning around and walked over to grab a life vest. The cool sand contorted to my stiff back. I rested my head on the makeshift pillow and watched long dark clouds. My mind wanted to run but

I fought the temptation and focused on the constant rolling waves. The presence of Kevin, safe and sleeping next to me, brought me back to our youth and the nights I stayed awake overthinking things important to a seven-year-old, with my carefree brother soundly sleeping in the bunk above me. I turned to look at him sleeping now and felt like a sleepless kid again.

* * *

Captain Dan finally turned off the flashlight and folded the nautical chart. I was still next to Kevin but could not sleep. Chase continued to chain smoke and watch the street from the boardwalk.

"You awake, Butch?" Captain Dan asked.

"Yeah."

"I know body language, learned how to read a man's thoughts in the Navy. Nobody could touch me on a card table."

I sat up and the cool wind awakened my senses. Kevin was snoring next to me. Captain Dan looked nervous, and he was never nervous.

"What are you thinking?"

"Thinking you boys had better have a plan. Your detective friend looks worried. He's watched that road for over an hour now. He'll abandon you two."

"What about the plane?"

"She'll be grounded for a day or maybe two at most."

The orange glow from a cigarette bounced in our direction. Captain Dan watched Chase as he approached. He nervously ran fingers through unkempt hair and laughed to himself. Captain Dan raised both eyebrows at me and folded his arms across a broad chest.

"Couple bullet holes shouldn't take long to repair," Chase said. "We need material, right?"

"Couple bullet holes?" Captain Dan said in a frustrated tone.

"We need to find another way to New Orleans," I said.

Chase shrugged and looked at Captain Dan. The two could not have been more opposite. The meticulous Navy veteran looked beyond frustrated. He could never have patience for a spontaneous rookie detective with nothing to lose.

"The only reason you're alive is because of Butch," Captain Dan said in a bellowing voice. "I don't know who or what is after us, but I'm willing to bet it has something to do with you. Am I right?"

Chase calmly lit another cigarette with the end of a butt and smiled. He had a smirk I remembered from my interrogation inside the belly of Miami PD. The only missing element was an overbearing Chief with drug money and corruption on his mind.

"I'll find us a car," Chase said and walked back toward the boardwalk.

"We don't have time for bullshit."

"Shouldn't we stay together?" I asked.

Chase ignored me and started walking up the boardwalk toward the road. I stood and watched him cross the street and disappear beyond the last streetlamp. The urge to follow faded with the sight of Captain Dan in front of me.

"Let him go," Captain Dan said with conviction. "You're better off without him right now."

"We need to stay together," I said. "He has half our resources."

"What resources?" Captain Dan asked as he closed the flight plan and tossed it in the sand next to Kevin. "Just let him go for a while."

He turned the flashlight off and walked over to where the seaplane was tied off on the beach. I watched him step up on one of the floats and crawl inside the cockpit. My eyes had adjusted, and I could see passed the seaplane where the black water rolled beneath a charcoal sky.

"Better watch him, Butch," Kevin said and stood up to brush the sand off his shorts. "We'll find Tatum Jones with or without Chase. Forget what he might want with him. We still need to clear your name."

Kevin slapped me on the shoulder and walked past me toward the water. I watched him clean his face and arms in the saltwater and considered running after Chase. The trust factor was still there for me, despite what had happened. Chase never would have showed me his abandoned house or told me about his murdered wife for no reason. He probably needs us more than we realize.

Kevin suddenly jumped inside a rolling wave before colliding with the next larger one. The phosphorescence sparkled when he hit the water. I turned to watch the road. Sea grapes and sea oats bundled together to form a barrier between the boardwalk and the dimly lit parking lot.

* * *

A car without headlights sped east down the road, engine roaring. It came to a screeching halt in the empty parking lot behind us with a cloud of exhaust streaming from the tailpipe, an eerie red glowing from the brake lights. I watched Kevin's eyes and knew he might have expected this.

"Let's go!" Chase said, leaning his head out the driver's seat. "Got us a loaner."

"From who?" Dan asked.

"Never mind that, Captain. Let's get out of here."

I helped them gather a few things and walked alongside the black sports car. Chase opened the passenger side door, and I was greeted with a cloud of cigarette smoke.

"Were you followed?" I asked.

"No, I stole this car from a condo parking lot up the street. Tatum's guys could never track us in this. The windows are even tinted."

"We need to get to New Orleans tonight," Kevin said as he sat down in the passenger seat. "We can't wait around here with the seaplane on the beach."

Captain Dan hesitated to get inside the car. He finally took a step back and shut the open door. Chase gave me a confused look and raised both hands to object.

"Let's go, Captain," Chase said. "We're marked here."

"I know a few guys, old floatplane pilots in town. They can help me get her working again. Go on without me."

"It's too dangerous," I said from the back seat.

"They'll kill you."

Captain Dan showed a humble smile and straightened his posture. His mind was clearly made up. He would never abandon his plane.

"Finish this, Kevin," Captain Dan said. "Do what you need to do and get yourself right again."

Kevin nodded and looked down at the floorboard. I could feel the emotion between them and knew that Captain Dan was the only person who could validate Kevin's actions. He was the father figure we needed now.

"I will, sir," Kevin said in a faint voice.

"Good." Captain Dan smiled. "Don't you boys worry about me. I survived Vietnam."

Chase lit a cigarette and extended his hand out the window. He shook hands with Captain Dan.

"Thank you for saving our lives. I owe you one, a big one."

Captain Dan finally let go and stepped away from the car. He smiled at me and turned away. I watched Kevin watching him and knew that we might never see him again.

I leaned back against the leather seat and closed my eyes. The car smelled of cheap cologne and the big-block engine roared as we sped west toward Interstate 10.

Chapter Thirteen

I woke up inside the stolen car to the sound of rolling waves along a nearby beach. Seagulls roamed for trash in front of a slow sunrise that highlighted the brown leather interior and sagging vinyl roof of this nineteen eighty something Camaro.

Chase and Kevin were still asleep and the hope that yesterday was a dream suddenly faded. I let them sleep and stepped out on the sand covered asphalt. A cool morning breeze opened my eyes as I walked away from the maroon sports car toward a quiet harbor that wrapped itself around a lone saloon named Peabody's. High-rise hotels freckled Pensacola's distant seascape along Via De Luna Drive.

A stout fisherman stood cutting mullet in the stern of his boat. He was alone in a crowded harbor and dressed in an oversized blue cabana shirt with a redfish pattern. I watched him finish the last two mullet and reach for an open bottle of rum atop a closed box of doughnuts. He took a long pull of rum before making eye contact with me.

"Something I can help you with?" he asked.

The answer was yes but I could not just come out and ask for a ride to New Orleans. A bilge pump turned on and the noise would be impossible to talk over. This forced me to walk toward his boat. I noticed the name, *Utopia*, painted in bold blue letters above twin inboards.

"Where can I get a cup of coffee," I asked.

"You look rough," he said. "Spring Break ended months ago."

I looked down at my filthy bare feet and wrinkled shorts. The front pocket of my gray shirt was full of sand, and I felt stubble on my chin.

"Let me buy you a coffee," I said.

"Why, I moved on to rum at sunrise," he said with a crooked smile. "New tactic I'm trying. Been skunked for almost three straight weeks. Bastards bite but nothing ever lands."

I used the sales tactic my father taught me when a subject denied an interview for a story. A short silence was long enough for this character. He avoided eye contact as he cleaned off the cutting board. I waited for him to cork the rum and join me on the dock.

"Fine, maybe I need a coffee this morning," he said. "You follow me."

"My treat," I said and followed.

The dock ended and a line of cut Bermuda grass lead us around a marina office and cluster of windmill palms toward the high-rise hotels that towered over seventy-foot Hatteras boats in a line of ten, bows pointed out and ready for the belly of the Gulf of Mexico beyond the shelf just a few miles out. I noticed a glass bottom tourist boat wedged between two of the white monsters.

"You coming?" he asked.

"Of course."

He held open a green door that led inside a foyer full of fishing mounts. A large King Mackerel caught my attention. The black line that ran away from daunting eyes and between mirror fins highlighted a body built for speed.

"Mine is bigger than that," he said walking by me.

I followed him inside and passed a dining area toward an empty barroom. A glass pot of coffee was on and half full. He walked around the bar and grabbed two ceramic mugs and handed me a white one with blue marlin painted on it.

"Are they open?" I asked. "Where's the bartender?"

"It's seven in the morning," he said pouring coffee.

I took a sip of black steaming coffee and found a seat on a barstool. He stayed behind the bar and leaned over to study his steaming cup.

"Are you a charter captain?"

He stood back from the bar with hands on hips. Blue bloodshot eyes connected with mine. A look of confusion followed.

"You asked me to have a cup of coffee with you. Cut the crap and say what you need to say."

"Is there a problem?"

"No problem. Let's start with names."

"Okay, I'm Butch."

"Good, now what did you want to ask me?"

"Who are you?"

"James."

The front door opened behind us, and I turned around. Kevin was alone and looked rough, even for his standards. I looked at James and nodded.

"He's with me, my brother, Kevin."

Kevin barreled toward the bar and sat down next to me without looking at either one of us. He was sweating and looked irritated. I waited for the uncomfortable silence to pass.

"Where's Chase?" I asked.

"Gone . . . again," Kevin said. "I got up after you left. Walked down to the pier to take a piss. Five minutes later, I'm watching Chase speeding out of the parking lot. Tried to stop him."

"What'd he say when you woke up?"

"He was sleeping when I walked to the pier."

Kevin turned to scan the empty dining room. James shrugged at his look of disappointment.

"What's your drink, Kevin?" James asked. "What will help?"

"Bourbon, scotch, anything but tequila. You work here?"

James smiled and reached behind the bar for a bottle of single-barrel bourbon. I waved away a rocks glass in frustration. My mind was on Chase and his habit of becoming less and less predictable.

"So now what, Kevin? We can't just sit around waiting for him."

"Have a taste of Kentucky's finest offering before answering your own question, Butch," James said as he poured three tall glasses."

Kevin raised both eyebrows at the strong but smooth bourbon. We collectively drank our glasses in one long swig and set them down on the oak bar. James had a wide smile now and his deep blue eyes were alive for the first time.

"Maybe he got a call from his guy in Miami. Maybe Chief Diggs caught up with us and he doesn't want us to know?"

"Stop making excuses," Kevin said holding his glass in anticipation of another shot of bourbon.

"Right, of course," James said and poured another round.

"I still trust him. His job is on the line—"

"My life is on the line," Kevin said. "What about Hailey? Hell, you could end up in jail without Chase covering your ass with the buried money. How much did you give him again? Hundred grand?"

"That's a lot of money," James said with arms folded. "You boys dealers?"

I decided not to respond to the questions and waited for my shot. The bourbon was easier going down the second time. This feeling always led to a third, fourth and fifth.

"Seriously, what's going on with you two?" James asked after his second shot. "You carrying that much on you now?"

"It's complicated," I said.

Kevin drank a third double shot of bourbon and stood up from the bar. He was noticeably upset with my silence. James froze between us. I shook my head as Kevin walked out through the front door.

"We don't really have time for an introduction," I said. "Is Utopia your boat?"

James finished his third double shot of bourbon and stared at me with glazed eyes. He reached down and pulled a flask out from his shorts pocket. A fourth shot came from that.

"You want my boat?" James leaned toward me with palms on the bar. "We just met."

"Let's take a walk. This place is too public for the conversation we need to have."

"You are running from something?"

"You could say that." I downed the remaining double shot of bourbon. "It's a little of both actually."

James walked from behind the bar and led me outside toward the harbor. He was a fast walker and acted more nervous than me. I followed him onto the stern of *Utopia*. We passed the cutting board and bloody bucket of chopped mullet, down a short ladder that led to a small dark kitchen in the galley.

"Have a seat."

"I'd rather stand for this."

"Suit yourself."

"When is your next charter? Busy time of year, right?"

His reaction was surprisingly sullen. I noticed a few revolvers on the countertop behind him. Open boxes of bullets were scattered in the sink.

"I'm kind of new to this charter fishing business down here. Business is kind of slow right now."

"How slow?"

He turned around and looked through a small refrigerator full of condiments and beer bottles. I watched his buzzed scalp bob and weave for a few moments before he decided on a can of lite pilsner beer. He cracked it open and smiled at the question.

"Let's just say, I'm sort of running from my own mess back in Kentucky." He took a long drink.

"Where about?"

"Louisville."

He set the beer down and walked toward a small couch to pick up an enormous King Mackerel. His eyes were alive again as he held it up for me to see in the dimly lit cabin.

"I won a local tournament a few months back. Decided to sell everything back home. Been chasing a dream ever since."

His King Mackerel was longer than the one on the foyer wall in the restaurant. It stood vertically on its tail and was taller than him. Must have weighed fifty pounds and every bit of 62" long.

"We need a ride to New Orleans. My brother and I are looking for a drug dealer from Miami."

"To buy or sell?" he said as he set the King Mackerel down on the round table between us.

"Kevin's girlfriend was recently murdered. This guy pulled the trigger."

"Did you go to the police?"

I laughed inside at the obvious question. Miami Police should have been the solution. Chief Diggs could end up being our biggest hurdle.

"They're in deep with this dealer. He practically owns the city."

"What's his name?" He finished the beer.

"Ever heard of Tatum Jones?"

"Tatum Jones?"

He stared at the filthy blue carpet on the cabin floor in deep thought. I noticed a change in his posture when realization hit. His body language told me everything.

"You mean, Tone?"

This was a strange coincidence. I shrugged and waited for more. His eyes moved side-to-side. He was noticeably working through the morning alcohol.

"I bought this boat from a dealer from Miami. Made me pay him in cash. Took thirty percent off the price. But it had to be cash. He said he worked for a guy named Tone. Must be the same guy, right?"

"I need to find Kevin," I said and climbed up the ladder.

"Wait, Butch, is it the same guy?"

I jumped down on the pier in stride and ran toward the parking lot. James yelled something that I could not understand in the growing distance between us. The side-plot of grass opened up to the same cluster of windmill palms. Kevin stood with hands on hips in the middle of the same empty parking lot. He watched as Chase rolled back into our lives. No beat-up Camaro this time. The long hood of a baby blue Lincoln Continental stopped at Kevin's feet. A burning cigar hung out the driver-side window and clung to long white fingertips. Chase Anderson gave me a nod and smiled at Kevin.

Chapter Fourteen

Chase bawled the baby blue Lincoln across the Alabama state line. Pensacola was a memory. The afternoon sun followed us like a spotlight. I watched the emerald coastline and thought about my encounter with James. *Utopia* was a good option to have on the way home. My dad believed that encounters with strangers happen for a reason, even when the reason takes time to understand. Kevin never agreed with this idea.

The open convertible made the silence acceptable as we drove. Kevin had not looked at Chase to this point. He sat shotgun with his eyes closed. Tension pulled at his face and shoulders.

"Are you going to tell us something?" I asked leaning forward.

"Tell you what?" Chase asked.

Kevin opened his eyes with wild hair blowing in the wind. He sat up and put both hands together at his nose. Chase focused on the road and leaned down to push in the lighter on the dashboard.

"We need to agree on something if this is ever going to last," Kevin said. "Just one thing."

"What's that?" Chase asked.

"No more disappearing acts. We need to communicate better and make sure that we're on the same page. Especially in New Orleans."

"Yeah, we thought you were gone," I said. "We were close to leaving Pensacola without you."

Chase drove toward a distant beach parking lot. He lit a new cigarette with one hand and steered the long convertible into an empty parking lot. I held onto the back seat to avoid the forward force from pushing me through the windshield.

"What did you think I was doing?"

"Who the hell knows with you," Kevin said leaning toward Chase. "One minute you're here, the next minute you're there. For all we knew, Chief Diggs was driving you back to Miami in handcuffs."

Chase let out a bellowing laugh and opened the long driver-side door. He walked around the car and leaned over the hood, palms down, and shook his head at both of us. Kevin gave me a familiar bullshit detector look and crossed his arms.

"You guys ever think about who's looking for us out here? Ever consider that maybe . . . maybe your Captain friend gave up information about the car we were driving to save his own ass?"

"He wouldn't do that," I said.

"Tatum Jones can get the hardest gangbanger to beg for mercy. I've watched him make powerful men piss their pants. He's an animal."

"No way," Kevin said. "Captain Dan is like a father. He'd die first."

"I don't know that about him. You never mentioned anything about him. Just assumed I would jump in his plane and entrust our lives with a senior citizen."

The enormity of the blue Gulf water distracted me. Chase looked away and raised both arms in frustration. Kevin rocked in his seat with arms crossed.

"Listen guys," Chase said still looking out at the beach. "My life depends on this case. And I was lost and ready to give up. But Butch showed up for a routine interrogation and everything changed. Kevin, I know the feeling you have every morning when you wake up, hoping your life is a bad dream. Some mornings, I'll keep my eyes closed and reach over in bed, hoping she's there. Looking for her warmth. But she's never there, and my hell just starts over for another day."

Chase turned back around with wet eyes and a closed posture. The burning cigarette hung from his left thumb and finger, his pitching hand.

"Without her . . . without baseball . . . what's the point? Catching this asshole is my reason for getting up in the morning. The reason for pulling myself off the empty bed."

Kevin shrugged and unlocked his arms. The wheels were turning in his head, and I could feel a change. He gave me a matter of fact look and nodded at Chase. For the first time, he appeared to trust him.

"I won't question you again. We need each other to finish this. So, let's finish it."

Chase wiped his eyes with the bottom of a filthy white shirt and punched the hood. He had new life and hurried around to the driver-side. He jumped in and the engine started. The big steering wheel guided us through the parking lot by a long row of newly planted sabal palms and I leaned forward against the winding road.

* * *

Rain covered Bourbon Street. People scampered about drinking beer and wine in the streets carelessly. I sat across from Chase on a square wooden table beneath the canopy of a rundown café.

"Who were the officers shooting at us?" I asked. "At Tarpon Marina?"

"Diggs sent them after me. It doesn't take long for them to react to a homicide." Chase flipped a toothpick around in his mouth.

"What homicide? It was self-defense."

A man painted with silver body paint stood still on the street corner. He stood below our table on the outside patio and stared at nothing. I watched the faces of the tourists react to him.

"They don't know that. Besides, you don't understand how things work down there."

"How do they work?"

"Chief Diggs is in Tone's pocket. So, when one of his own detectives ends up killing one of Tone's brothers, there tends to be a chain reaction."

Chase kept looking and smiling at someone behind me. I turned in my seat and noticed two younger looking brunettes at a window table inside the café. They smiled at us and gently waved.

I turned back around to face an approaching waitress. She set a dozen steamed clams on the table. Chase wasted no time. He reached for one and scooped the clam from its shell with a small fork and drowned it in melted butter sauce.

"There you go, boys," she said. "Jambalaya should be up soon."

"What do you think?" Chase asked smiling before he ate the clam.

"I haven't had one yet," I said and grabbed a clamshell.

I used a small fork to scoop out the clam and held it in the melted butter before eating it.

"Not the food, Butch. What about those two?"

He nodded at the two girls behind me. I was surprised at how easily he was distracted. We were not in New Orleans for the attractions.

"Let's stick to the reason we're here."

"Be right back."

Chase quickly ate another clam and stood up from the table. He picked up his cup of coffee and walked inside the café. Minutes later, he sat back down and went back to eating clams. He shook his head and smiled about something.

"Where'd you go, Chase?"

"Made a phone call to one of my guys at the department."

"Who?"

"Someone we can trust. He's calling back in about fifteen minutes."

"What did you . . . why did you call?"

"Find out what's happened since we left. You know . . . see if Tone showed up on the front page or something."

"What if this guy gives us up? Did you tell him we're in New Orleans?"

"Relax, Butch. He owes me more than a few favors. We need something to go on here. You can't expect to bump into Tone on Bourbon Street tonight. We need a contact person. A lead, someone he might know up here. That's what he's checking."

"Who would they know in New Orleans?"

"Precincts help each other out."

"How long did he say?"

"Maybe twenty-minutes, just a couple of phone calls."

Chase ate another clam and waved at the girls behind me. I wondered when Kevin would show up. He had been gone for over an hour now.

"Kevin should be back soon."

"Yeah, hopefully," Chase said. "I'll be right back."

* * *

Twenty minutes turned into an hour and Chase had disappeared with his new friends. I walked alone down a dark cobblestone street inside the French Quarter. The constant push from strip club bouncers handing out free drink coupons was a bit overwhelming. Bourbon Street has an unexplainable allure but so much of it reminds me of everything that is wrong with Key West. The main differences between them were surrounding seascapes and the deep blue Gulf Stream, compared to a murky bayou and brown Mississippi River. I would take Key West every time.

An elderly man caught my attention on the sidewalk and motioned me over. He stood in silence with arms crossed in front of a half dozen beer kegs and boxes of red plastic cups. The structure behind him protruded from the brownstone building and had been formed with cheap plywood and painted a dirty white that blended in with the dirty street. I approached the unstable structure and waited for the man to pump the keg and fill one of the red cups.

"Enjoying yourself are you now?" the man asked with bare gums. "Forget that other crap . . . you hear me?" He pulled black greased bangs away from his face and handed me a cup of mostly foam. "Two dollars. Three for one more."

The first cup of watered-down light beer was easy. I agreed on a second one and handed the man a hundred-dollar bill. His dark eyes grew wide with excitement.

"Keep the change," I said. "Find a bed to sleep in tonight."

"God bless you!" the man said and poured another foam filled beer. "Double fisted now, right?"

He pulled a cigar box from under a rocking chair and put the money in it. His spirit was alive at the possibilities that come with unexpected money. It reminded me of the first time I found the buried money that ultimately brought me to Chase Anderson.

"Thank you so much . . . thank you thank you."

I nodded and walked away before being tempted to drink more beer. The streets began to fill with locals and tourists. I walked through bunches of obnoxious people by pockets of live music changing sounds every block or so. There was jazz and classic rock mixed in with some reggae. I eventually made it back to the same café where I left Chase. The sun was setting, and I began to wonder about Kevin.

Chase was nowhere to be found and the café was closing soon for the evening. I walked next door to a jazz bar. Trumpets played inside and small crowds gathered around glowing candles on circular tables. A young musician stood on a dimly lit stage with dark cheeks puffing and sweat rolling off his round head. The sounds were soothing and real. I made eye contact with a brunette cocktail waitress and waved her over.

"Where have you been?" Chase asked and grabbed me around the neck. He was laughing uncontrollably. "Guy's unreal—" his voice was overpowered by the trumpet.

"Where in the hell did you go?" I asked and noticed one of the girls from the café standing next to him, smiling. "Can you excuse us?"

I pulled Chase away from the bar. He turned and whispered something to the girl and followed me outside.

Herds of people pushed through the street now. Chase walked with me near an alley entrance. The smell of trash and stale beer were pungent and distracted our conversation.

"Did they call, Chase?"

"Silly question."

Chase lit a match just to watch it burn. The light reflected off his sunglasses. His smug smile was infuriating.

"Who's our source then?"

"I finally got a name and number. We'll see them tomorrow. I just need some time away to clear my mind."

"Fine. Do what you have to tonight. But tomorrow . . . you know what I mean. We must call this person. Maybe find one of his dealers or something?"

"Street investigation? Didn't know you beat writers did those things. Thought it was all desk and computer work."

Chase laughed at his own sarcasm before pulling his gun from its holster and handing it to me.

"Wrong weapon tonight. Take this until tomorrow," Chase said and looked around at the people on the street. "In case something comes up."

"Meet us at the car, say around seven tomorrow morning?"

"Better make it eight."

"Right."

"Where is Kevin anyway?"

I shrugged and placed the gun in my pants pocket. The crowded street pulled Chase and he pushed his way to the bar entrance where the girl waited. He turned his head with a reassuring look. I nodded and walked away.

Chapter Fifteen

I watched the Mississippi River for the first time. It was dark and hidden the night before. Brown flowing water pushed floating tree trunks along wide riverbanks. The powerful combination of rivers barreled southbound for an encounter with blue Gulf waters.

I stood under a streetlamp and called my office. There was no answer. Two street thugs exchanged something for something else near the riverbank. The gray hooded one walked away toward Bourbon Street, while the one wearing sunglasses with an afro-pick found a seat on a wooden bench. He counted large stacks of money. A third person walked up from the shadows of a large bridge underpass and approached the one counting money. A revolver hung from his grasp. The tattoos on his arms and neck were familiar from a short distance. They stood facing one another while the constant river flowed yards away. I wondered what they were talking about.

My cell rang and the one with the revolver noticed me standing there. I answered it. "Hello."

"Butch," a voice said.

"Who is this?" I asked but remained focused on the one watching me.

"I can only protect your ass for so long," Dudas spoke fast, "Chief Diggs has been here a few times demanding answers. He mentioned that Chase Anderson is the suspect in a big narcotics cover-up. You know anything about him being involved?"

"I thought we had this conversation."

I stopped talking as the one with the revolver approached me. Reflective sunglasses blocked eye contact between us.

"Hang up," he said and looked down at the gun.

"Give me something that resembles a feature story. I need something to cover your ass. Miami PD thinks you're out of town on assignment. I told them you were covering a story for me in Miami. This could be huge. You could bring down an empire—"

I hung up the phone and stared at my own reflection in his sunglasses. He looked familiar even without seeing his eyes. Everything about him resembled Tatum Jones. But that would be impossible. How could I have found him? Or did he find me first?

"Where's your cop friend?" he asked and looked away toward an empty street corner.

A taxicab slowed to a stop not far from us. He placed the revolver in his pants pocket and turned away from me. I pretended to use my cell phone again.

"Act cool, Butch," he said in a whisper. "You make a move and I'll kill you."

The cab driver honked three times then sped away. I watched the yellow lights move through traffic and bend out of sight.

"Come with me," he said and turned to face me again. "I need to do a few things first."

"Why did you kill those two at the gas station?" I asked without thinking.

"Why do you think?" He removed the sunglasses to reveal the teardrop tattoo under his right eye. "Survival, that's the game." He kissed a gold cross that hung around his neck. "Something your cracker ass friend knows nothing about."

"I know your history with Chase. But I'm here because of someone else."

"Been tracking y'all since Tampa." He smiled. "These eyes are everywhere. Don't play this off as a coincidence. Could've blasted you both earlier."

"Why didn't you?"

"Chief Diggs wants a clean kill. He doesn't want this precinct involved. Before you know it, CNN and FOX show up to create a storyline about feuding police departments. You know, Miami versus New Orleans."

"What now?"

"Your ass stays with me until I get my prize."

I thought about leaving but knew I had to stay calm. My choices were limited. Hopefully, Kevin finds his way around Tatum Jones.

"Let's take a walk, Butch."

I followed Tatum across the street toward a parked car and wondered when Chase would arrive. Tatum led me down a cobblestone street toward another side street. The repugnant smell of vomit and garbage lingered on both sides. I covered my nose and followed him through an area of New Orleans tourists would never know about. Desperate looking people would step aside or look away when Tatum walked by them. Their wide eyes fixated on me, an easy target.

"Where are we going?"

"No questions."

We both stopped at the end of an alley where two women stood by a dumpster. They were dressed in tight clothes and wore heavy red lipstick.

"Let me handle my employees for a minute," Tatum said and motioned for me to stand back as he approached them. "They trippin."

He pulled a wad of money out of a purse and one of them started crying about something. Her frail friend rubbed her shoulders and made a shushing sound in her ear. The two of them smelled of body-odor and cigarettes. Both had bleached blonde hair and fake breasts. Mascara started to run down the side of her battered face.

"Who takes care of you? Huh?" Tatum asked and counted a stack of wrinkled twenty-dollar bills. "Don't you ever do that again, Lovell. You ever do that again your ass is going to the dogs! You hear me, woman?" He shoved the money in his pocket and turned to walk away. "Let's go, Butch. Damn."

"Sorry, Tone. We know about June and everything," her friend said and lit a joint with shaking hands. "We want no trouble. We know you mean business." She began to cough uncontrollably.

Neither woman acknowledged me standing there. I was like a ghost. A sick feeling ripped through my stomach. *What wasted lives.*

"Don't have much time before Chase gets back," Tatum said as we hurried out to the street.

"How do you know when he's coming back?"

"Sent a few of my ladies his way."

"Hookers?"

"What did you think?"

"We just got here last night. How'd you know we were here?"

Tatum smiled and the teardrop tattoo rose on his narrow cheekbone. I ignored his carefree mood and pulled a small notepad and pen out from my pants pocket and adjusted the nine-millimeter gun that pressed against the small of my back.

"Are you going to interview me, Butch?"

"What else do you know about me?"

"Where should I start?"

I knew everything was about to change. Chase must have known that Tatum could find us first. His nervousness and lack of trust for Captain Dan made sense now, more than before, no wonder he kept changing stolen cars.

"You boys had a lot of nerve shooting up my house," he said with a change in attitude. "You killed one of my partners. Killed June Bug."

Tatum removed his sunglasses. Chestnut brown eyes stared through me. He grabbed a pack of rolling papers from his coat pocket.

"Unlucky, I guess."

"What are you doing here, Butch? I could have killed you this morning, but I needed to know a few things first."

"Know what?"

"Hold up," Tatum said and eased inside a voodoo coffee house without hesitation. I found a seat on the steps of an old apartment building surrounded by worn brick buildings and wrote some questions in my notepad. The surrounding structures were old and cracking with trash in the streets and people standing on street corners, silent and aware of everything around them. I felt uncomfortable sitting down.

Warm air flushed out the awful odors and river smell. The Mississippi River flowed south along scarcely vegetated banks. I watched an elderly man bait the hook of a cane pole and toss the line out into the strong current. A group of about ten street thugs noticed him sitting there and one made a hand gesture at him as Tatum walked out of the coffee house with a steaming cup of coffee. He found a seat on the step next to me.

"Just needed my coffee," Tatum said and looked over at the group and made a hand signal at the one who'd noticed me first. "Forget them. They think you're squatting for powder." He held the cup up to his nose and inhaled the aroma.

"Cocaine?" I asked. "Thought you dealt heroin?"

"Depends on the market." He set a gun down on the step in front of him and sipped from the cup with both hands. "Best coffee around here, man. You know, June Bug was a serious coffee drinker. He always had some foreign shit you wouldn't believe, fair trade only. Bastard was fickle about it. Never find his ass sitting in a Starbucks. Hell, he drank coffee at midnight most nights." He stopped drinking and poured the coffee along the bottom step and tossed the cup down. "My brother in arms." He rubbed his eyes and dropped his head.

I knew what was coming next and thought about going for the gun now but knew what would happen if I did. The group on the corner was not there by mistake. I reminded myself that he has a network of people guarding him and scrambled through the notepad to appear busy.

"What about that politician from Miami?"

"What about him?"

"Who was he?"

"Bastard wasn't worth the air he breathed. He evicted some of my family from their apartments without warning. Brought the police in on a Sunday morning before church and ran them out."

"But why—"

"They're my people. Someone needs to protect them from that racist asshole. Just like your friend, bastard deserves what's coming to him. He'll have his day of judgment for what he did . . . you wait."

"What about you? What about the lives you ruin with your business? What's the difference?"

"Ruin lives? I save lives daily. Feed my people, clothe them, give them a place to sleep. What do you mean, ruin lives?"

"Selling an addiction isn't real work. You're killing people."

"Not the way I do it."

"You ruined my brother's life too. And for what?"

"Remember, I'm a businessman, CEO and shit. This is my office out here." he said and raised his arms toward the street. "I got middle management over there, salesmen selling a good clean product from here to Miami."

I looked around at the misery in the streets, kids with no fathers holding small clear bags of cocaine in their socks, thousands of dollars in their pockets. Dropouts, bastards, gang bangers, cowards with a pack mentality, kids who have never taken a punch, too scared to fight with their knuckles because that is who raised them. Cowards and thugs with one thing in mind, getting high at any cost until the cost is too much to live.

"Do you realize what heroin can do to a person?" I asked but felt uncomfortable asking questions now. The fear of being shot had slipped away.

"Hell yeah . . . took my father's life, made my baby brother hang himself, and turned my only sister into a whore."

His answer was real, and I had not considered his life in all of this. I had presumed he was merely a gangbanger. Dealing crack for Tatum was as normal as watching baseball or going to the movies for me.

"I know about you and Chief Diggs."

"So, what," Tatum said and squashed the coffee cup with his foot. "Chase, Kevin, and you are dead men either way."

"How long have you been on the inside?" I asked as I scanned the notepad.

"Money can move mountains," Tatum said smiling. "Women and drugs blow up the same mountains."

"You bought him then."

"You think I'm proud of my way of life? You think I want to live this way?"

He jumped down from the steps to the street and kicked over a trashcan, spilling beer bottles and used diapers. I was surprised at this reaction. Maybe Chief Diggs struck a nerve inside him. Maybe his coolness was just deception.

"Maybe."

"What do you know about any of it, Butch? You've never seen a man die after just one hit. Never watched a fourteen-year-old girl light a glass pipe in one hand and hold a crying baby in the other."

Tatum acknowledged the revolver on the steps at my feet and nodded for me to pick it up. For a moment, I'd forgotten about it.

"Chase is a coward. He's just a yellow ass cop—"

"Watch it, Tone!" someone yelled out from the street corner.

A fist came across Tatum's chin before he could react. He fell hard to the cement. Chase had sucker-punched him and was now straddling him and dropping blow after blow across his face with a fierce quickness.

"Hold up, white boy!" a voice shouted before a charge of strangers hurried toward the scene.

I sat awestruck. One blow after another rained down across Tatum's face. Blood splattered on Chase's white shirt. He stopped punching just as the first one came at him with a wooden baseball bat. He dodged an attempted blow to his head and stepped back before drawing a pistol from an ankle holster. The sound of multiple guns being cocked, and magazines loaded came from the posse of street thugs.

"You wanna hang 'im up and bar-b-q his pale ass?" another one said wearing a black vest and blue headband.

"Step away from Tone and get your ass over there next to your partner," a third attacker said through gold teeth and a white towel draped around his neck. His black eyebrows had shaved lines in them, and a handlebar mustache was bushy across his dark face.

"You still have it, Butch?" Tatum struggled to talk.

"Yeah," I said.

Tatum rolled around in his own blood, and I watched him feel for his teeth. He pushed Chase off his chest and slowly sat up. The street turned silent. Everyone stopped moving.

"Don't even think about it, cuz," Tatum said looking at me. "You shoot six of us and the other four gonna string your ass up."

"Don't do anything until I do. Understand?" Chase said and stepped up and kicked Tatum in his ribcage. "Think you can run the police? What's wrong? I'm a cop . . . why don't you tell me what to do?"

"You're a pig?" someone said holding an empty trashcan. "Catch this cop!" another one sidestepped and threw it at Chase who guided it away with his free hand and stepped back from the group. He stopped when our shoulders were touching. We were surrounded.

"Come on, Tone," someone wearing an NBA jersey said, helping Tatum to his feet. "We got you."

The rest of the group inched closer to us with guns drawn. Tatum hobbled away from the scene toward a black SUV with twenty-inch rims and tinted windows. The driver hurried out, gold chains bouncing around his neck, and helped his injured leader inside the back seat.

Chase stepped away from the insurgent group and kept his aim on Tatum without changing his focus. The small crowd began to grow around us as I watched his SUV turn down an alley. Our mark was gone.

"You all die . . . regardless," Chase said in a faint voice.

"I take that bet, cracker," someone shouted back.

"We deal with death every day, son. You're no different."

The NBA jersey stepped in front of the crowd and pointed a semi-automatic assault rifle inches from Chase. Police sirens interrupted everything. They sounded distant but drew closer by the second. Chase invited the distraction and quickly pulled his police badge out and held it in the face of his newest adversary. The group erupted in laughter.

"You're all under arrest for attempted assault on a police officer," Chase said. "You have the right to remain silent."

Their laughter increased the more serious Chase sounded. He gave me a nod and mouthed the word, run. But I felt stuck. My feet seemed cemented to the filthy concrete. I looked at the scene and the old man who'd stopped fishing to watch us standing here. The crowd on the street turned silent as the sirens drew nearer. Their faces shared the same surprised reaction, their eyes upon us, looking very human for the first time. Chase made another nod at me.

"Back up has arrived, gentlemen," Chase said. "Please set your firearms down, hands up where I can see them. You're all going to jail."

Police cruisers screeched around the corner. Chase spit his toothpick in the face of the man holding the assault rifle then fired two shots in the air, prompting everyone on the street to fall to the ground for cover.

"Why are you still here, Butch?" Chase asked and pushed me toward the alley behind us.

I got my feet back and sprinted ahead of him down the same alley that Tatum walked me through earlier. The familiar smells of vomit and trash hit me like a sledge. Multiple gunshots sounded from the street behind us.

"Move, Butch. They're gaining on us."

He fired two more shots in the air. Return fire followed. Bullets shot by us, sparking against the brick walls and pelting a green dumpster.

"Butch!"

I stopped to turn around. Chase ran toward me holding his shoulder. He motioned for me to keep moving. I turned and sprinted again toward the street and immediately turned left and continued moving. I stopped at the next intersection on the corner near the same coffee stand Tatum had gone into that morning. Chase was nowhere in sight. People walked along the French Quarter without worry. Window shoppers dominated the sidewalks. The scene I ran from was invisible to everyone else. A proprietor watered pink and yellow flowers in wooden boxes next to where I stood catching my breath.

Minutes went by and still no Chase. I adjusted the nine-millimeter and decided to walk back the way I came. Heavy footsteps sounded around the corner.

"Butch! Go . . . come on . . . go," Chase said sprinting past me. Blood covered his white shirt near the right shoulder, and his face had been bloodied too. "Hurry up. Let's go!"

Relieved that he was alive, I pushed off the building and sprinted after him. His body leaned low at the injured shoulder and streaks of blood painted his spiked blonde hair.

I finally caught up to Chase before the keg stand on Bourbon Street. The old drunkard still sat on his stool and drank beer. He smiled at me and lifted a plastic cup. I ran up the street toward the parked Lincoln Continental. The uncertainty of Tatum lingered. We needed to find Kevin as soon as possible. Tatum's entire crew knew us now.

A late evening thunderstorm followed us along the Mississippi coastline down by Gulf Shores Alabama. Chase had passed out in the passenger seat with blood seeping through his shirt at the shoulder. I weaved through traffic along interstate ten and scanned the roadside for a blue hospital sign. The threat of being followed was real. I hoped Captain Dan was still stuck in Pensacola. Chase and I were lucky to be alive.

"Pull over, Butch," Chase said in a faint voice. "I need to get out of this convertible and smoke a cigarette."

"You need a hospital."

"Come on, man. I need to get out for a minute."

I swerved over to the slow lane and flipped the hazard lights on before pulling off the highway onto the grass. A semi screamed by before he opened the door and stumbled out.

"Right here is fine," Chase said and vomited in the grass.

"Can you make it to Pensacola?" I asked.

"Do I have a choice?"

"You need a doctor."

"Of course, I need a doctor. But that would require a normal situation."

"We're about an hour away from the seaplane."

"You think he waited for us?"

"I hope."

"What if he didn't?" Chase asked through a cough. "What if the plane's still down?"

He slammed the door shut and sat back in the seat gasping to catch his breath. I waited for a group of cars to pass and sped up to re-join the flow of traffic. Our big engine roared through darkness.

"Which one shot me anyway?" Chase asked.

"Not sure. There were too many of them with guns."

I sped up to pass and the rain fell harder now. The windshield wipers were not working well, and we were both getting soaked.

"Just get me to Pensacola, Butch, and I'll figure this out from there. Get me close to where we left the seaplane, and I can fix this. Damn this rain. Can't even light a cigarette."

"Did you ever speak to your contact?"

"No, but you should call Dudas again for an update. See if he has heard anything from Chief Diggs or from one of Tatum's guys for that matter."

"I tried a few hours ago. When you were with the hookers."

"They weren't hookers."

"Tatum said they were hookers. And he's been tracking us since we left Pedro Island. Followed us to Pensacola and New Orleans."

"What about Kevin?"

"He has no idea what happened or where we are."

"Call his cell."

"I will once we get you to a hospital. He'll be able to catch up with us in Pensacola."

"He'll be pissed, right?"

"What do you think?"

I tried to call Kevin three times with no answer. Chase smiled at my obvious concern for Kevin's safety and stopped talking. He put an unlit cigarette in his mouth and closed his eyes. I continued to drive fast through the heavy downpour.

The coastline was dark and there was no moon. I thought about Hailey for the first time today and wondered what she was doing at this very moment, probably something normal. Normal would be nice, just a normal night, boring and calm. But it was never boring and calm with her.

The gray horizon spread out across a flat coastline. Thunderclouds rumbled overhead and a southeasterly wind shook the palmettos and pine trees that lined the interstate. We sped beneath an overpass around a pack of semitrucks. The eastbound side of the road was empty ahead with faint red car lights in the distance. I checked the review mirror every minute or so to be sure no one had followed. I felt lucky to be alive and hoped Kevin's sanity would last until tomorrow. Lack of sleep had finally caught up with me. I sat back and closed my eyes.

Chapter Sixteen

A school of yellow jacks darted between coral ten fathoms deep and the sprawl of gray sand surrounded black rocks. I held on to a rock with one hand and a spear gun and bag of fish with the other. The shadow from a giant grouper moved below me before I swam toward the beach.

Hailey lay out-stretched on a towel near a cluster of sea oats, farther down the beach. Three-foot waves pushed me through the deeper water until I stood chest high in the smooth ripple of sand. I waded toward the shore as thunderclouds rumbled in the distance.

"Are you awake?" I asked as I approached her lying there. After placing the bag of red snapper in the cooler, I dried off with a towel.

"I'm awake," she said and sat up on both elbows. "What time are we meeting them for dinner?"

"I'm supposed to call when we get back to your place." I dried my hands before grabbing the camera and pulled off the lens cover. She stood up from the beach towel and folded her arms. "Let me get a shot of this."

"Just make this quick, Butch."

She dropped her arms and smiled. I snapped a shot of her with a backdrop of the island lighthouse, sea oats, thunderclouds, and sugar-sand.

"Perfect."

"Hurry up—"

"Butch? We're heading home . . . come on, wake up."

I woke to someone pushing my shoulder. The feel of worn leather pressed against my bare back. The green and blue seascape was a blur from the backseat window of a different stolen car. This one was compact and smelled like a chimney. The worn vinyl ceiling shook with the wind.

"Where the hell are we?" I asked and sat up to watch the empty road through a filthy windshield. Chase turned and smiled with a newly lit cigarette in the side of his mouth.

"You're a trooper, Butch. We haven't stopped since New Orleans."

"Did you hear from Kevin?"

"No. You've been out for a few hours."

"How far are we from Captain Dan?"

Chase pulled the car off the interstate into a rest stop. I found my shirt in a pile behind the driver's seat and put it on. Chase pulled the roll of hundred dollar bills out and counted it.

"We needed to wait for Kevin. This doesn't work without him."

"Relax. I left a voicemail for Dudas. He knows we're fine. And he knows to tell Kevin to meet us at your office in a few days."

"What about your shoulder?"

"I met this blonde firecracker behind a truck stop while you were sleeping. She wrapped my shoulder with an old shirt and gave me a bottle of painkillers. The bullet must have gone straight through."

"Are you serious? What about the Continental?"

"Thought we needed an upgrade. Besides, Tatum knows that car."

"You break the law more than any cop I've ever met."

"You're no Saint yourself. What about all this money?"

"I'm not talking about that without an attorney."

"Exactly."

I needed a minute alone and stepped outside of the stolen car and walked toward the bathroom area of the rest stop. Chase cleared his throat behind me and stretched his healthy arm. I ignored him and walked inside. An enormous map of Florida hung on the wall with hundreds of tourist brochures stacked along both sides. The big red arrow on the map pointed directly at Destin.

I ran my finger back along interstate ten through Pensacola then down the axis highway leading to where Captain Dan had landed the seaplane the night before. I had a feeling that he was still there and hurried back outside.

"Over here, Butch. Dudas wants to talk to you," Chase said.

"Dudas," I said.

"Are you out of your mind, Sands?" Dudas yelled.

"Have you heard from Hailey?"

The line was silent for a time. I could hear heavy breathing followed by a crunching sound. He was eating pretzels or something.

"Chase calls me about a killer, and you're concerned about Hailey, who is out of the country right now. Seriously?"

"I need you to call Tarpon Marina and ask about Captain Dan's seaplane. See if he returned yet."

"You do realize a killer is chasing you—"

I handed the phone back to Chase and walked toward the parking lot.

"Which car is ours?" I asked.

"That one over there," Chase said and pointed at a Fleetwood Cadillac parked halfway up on the sidewalk.

"I didn't realize it was a Cadillac," I said.

"Some old man just went inside his house and left the key in the ignition," Chase said and covered the phone. "What about your boss?"

"You called him. Just hang up. We'll be there in what, four hours?"

"Give me a minute, Butch. It's unlocked."

Chase ended the call and darted inside toward the bathrooms. I sat on the hood of the stolen car and rubbed my now aching temples. I thought about the time I spent with Tatum in New Orleans, and how similar he was to guys I'd counseled during summers in college, working at a half-way house in Northern Kentucky. The circumstances had been quite different, but the dialogue was nearly the same. Most had no father. Many had no sense of family, that *"me against the world"* mentality that so many believed was their only chance for survival. The look in their eyes filled with hopelessness and discouragement. The way they spoke of the penitentiary as a birthright.

It all sounded the same. But nothing seemed to change fast enough. They'll kill themselves; I remembered a skinhead named Cecil say once during a counseling session. I remembered his rap sheet. Five pages filled with child abuse, armed robbery, and cocaine possession. I remembered the stillness of his light-blue eyes when he spoke of them as animals, and the confusion that made him speechless when posed the simplest of questions, why? Why were they animals? Why are they different from you? He never had an answer for why.

I leaned back on the hood and closed my eyes and tried to think about anything else. The past forty-eight hours were a blur. I tried to think about Hailey and her happiness for her sister's wedding. The image set in briefly before the ignition turned and the engine rumbled beneath me.

My cell phone vibrated as I sat up. I pulled it out. Kevin was calling.

"Kevin, where are you?"

"Pensacola. Where are you?"

"Where?"

"Standing in the stern of Utopia at the same marina I found James."

"We're on our way."

I closed the phone and hurried inside the big Cadillac. Chase reacted to someone running toward us and dropped the car in reverse. He spun it around and floored it toward the interstate.

"Go west," I said.

"West?" he said looking through the rearview. "What the hell for?"

* * *

Chase pulled through the same parking lot in front of the same Pensacola Marina we left the day before. I hurried out and ran through the same Bermuda grass toward the same dock. James was standing over the same cutting board filleting red snapper.

"James," I said and stopped to catch my breath. "Where's Kevin?"

"Inside at the bar," James said. "He's in rough shape."

"What happened?"

"You should ask him."

I nodded and turned to walk toward the same bar. Inside, I found Chase sitting at the bar next to Kevin. His eyes were red with excitement.

"Kev," I said as I walked over to join them. "When did you get here?"

"What the hell happened last night?" Chase asked. "You never came back to the restaurant."

"I came back," Kevin said staring at the ice in his glass. "Watched you leave with those two hookers."

Chase looked at me with raised eyebrows. He knew it was an error in judgment but was not thinking at the time. I watched him contemplating the idea that he had abandoned us at the worst possible time.

"You left my brother alone with a killer. I followed them through back alleys and watched them almost kill you both."

Chase tossed a pack of cigarettes on the bar and lit one. Kevin grabbed one and looked at me. The tension was growing. I knew my brother was pissed.

"This is our fight," Kevin said as he lit the cigarette. "Tatum ruined our lives. Butch doesn't even belong here. His life shouldn't be compromised because of an error in judgment. He's still got a life to live after this bullshit is over."

"Butch would be in jail right now, if not for me. I stopped it because I believed his story."

"And because he found your mark," Kevin said as he reached across the bar for a half-empty bottle of bourbon. "Without us, you're still just a yes man for one of the most corrupt police departments in the country. Chief Diggs would still be kissing the ass of the dealer that ruined your life in one moment."

A long silence followed. Kevin poured himself a double. Chase pulled his own rocks glass from a sink and slid it down the bar until it clanked against the bourbon bottle.

"Pour me one, too," Chase said.

Kevin poured his drink, and they drank the bourbon simultaneously. I sat back and waited for a reaction from Chase. Kevin set his glass down and leaned over the bar with both elbows. Chase slammed his glass and stood from the bar.

"Kevin!" a familiar voice sounded from the front of the bar. "We need to go now. I just got the call."

Kevin looked at me with newfound confidence and sprang from the bar. He hurried toward the front door where James waited in his flamingo button down, too small for his thick shoulders and neck. James waved us over and followed Kevin outside toward the dock. Chase looked concerned.

"Who called him, Butch?"

Before I could guess, gunshots sounded outside. I stopped at the door. Chase paused behind me and pulled out the .44 magnum. We both waited for another gunshot that never came. Complete silence followed.

"Stay inside," Chase said and leaned against the open door.

I instantly thought the worst. Kevin was gone. Chase looked around the door. His shoulders fell and the tension was gone from his body. Rumbling sounds from multiple outboard engines came from the marina.

"Is it . . . can you see Kevin?" I asked. "Say something."

Chase put the gun away and walked outside shaking his head. I followed him out but stopped at the front step. James lay motionless in the Bermuda grass. He had been shot three times in the chest. Circles of blood covered pink flamingos across the front of his tight shirt. A few yards away, Kevin stood on the bow of *Utopia* holding a spear gun. A dark-skinned man lay in a pool of blood on the dock before him. The end of a metal trident spear stuck out mid-back. I recognized the dead man's face from the night before in New Orleans.

"Who's that?" Chase said pointing at the dead man on the dock.

"Tatum sent him down here to collect money from one of his Panhandle dealers," Kevin said. "Too bad though, James seemed like a good guy."

"James works for Tatum?" I asked.

"Worked," Chase said and lit a cigarette. "Who else did he send down?"

"One of Tatum's dealers," Kevin said. "Wouldn't say his name though."

"Well, you can guarantee there'll be about ten of them within a few hours of this asshole not answering his phone. Probably sooner than that."

Chase walked down to the dock and rolled the dead man over. He ignored the open eyes and pulled a gangster roll of hundred-dollar bills from his pants pocket. I looked at Kevin and shook my head. He had a look of frustration. I knew this was getting out of control, even for him.

"Let's get South boys," Chase said and jumped in the stern of *Utopia*. "Come on, Butch. We need to reset."

"We're not going to Miami," I said.

"Who said anything about Miami?" Chase sat in the captain's chair.

I looked down at James and felt sorry for his wasted life. He was a trustworthy person with bad luck. People were put in our path for a reason. His decision to leave everything in Louisville for a better life along the Gulf Coast led to his *utopia*. Some people spend a lifetime looking for theirs.

Chapter Seventeen

Dudas blocked the doorway of the news building. Two police officers stood outside beneath the awning next to the dimly lit porch light. The street behind them was dark and silent. I listened to them question Dudas about our whereabouts. The conversation lasted about ten minutes before Dudas finally closed the door on them.

The air-conditioner had not worked in weeks and the room was hot and humid. I crawled out from under Carla's desk and watched the officers drive away through the front window. Chase and Kevin walked out from Dudas' office, each smoking a Cuban cigar. The white bandage around Chase's shoulder was soaked in blood but it did not seem to bother him.

"You're soaked in blood," Dudas said.

"I can't figure out why they didn't ask about Chase," I said and wiped sweat from my forehead. "Neither of them has a clue about anything."

"And those two were handpicked by Chief Diggs," Chase said and flipped ash on the floor. "I swear he hires dumb just to feel smart."

"Maybe that's why he hired Chase," Kevin said looking out the window.

"Excellent point, Kev," Dudas said smiling at Chase. "Feels weird to have to hide on this island of all places, we're not even safe at home."

"Listen, Chase. You'd better see a doctor about that shoulder," Dudas said.

"No worries, I can handle myself."

Dudas shook his head and walked into the kitchen to make a pot of coffee. I found a seat and felt my leg. It did not hurt for the first time since the gas station.

"We couldn't hear your conversation from your office," Kevin said. "What did they say?"

"I just told them you hadn't been here for at least a week. Not since you drove Butch to Miami."

"What about me?" Chase asked and puffed smoke.

"You're the reason they're in this mess."

"I've been protecting them!" Chase said, throwing the cigar on the floor. "Same damn thing in New Orleans. How do you think this happened?" Chase pointed at his blood-soiled shirt.

"I'm only with this guy because of Butch," Kevin said pointing at Chase. "Sure, we all have our reasons for chasing Tatum Jones. But Butch isn't going to jail. Not ever."

"Jail," Dudas said with raised eyebrows. "What's he talking about?"

I made eye contact with Chase and sighed. He shrugged and turned away from the group. Dudas looked confused and pissed at the same time.

"You know, I wanted to let this thing play out at first," Chase said with folded arms and narrowed eyes. "If I remember correctly, Kevin was the one without any patience."

"I never needed you. But when you threatened my brother, I never had another choice. This is my issue. He killed Rose—"

"He had Grace killed, too." Chase was visibly upset. "You're not the only one with something to prove."

"You better wait here until morning and find a doctor," Dudas said. "I could call one tonight for that matter."

"I'm not listening to this bullshit," Chase said and smirked at me before walking toward the front door. "You know how to reach me."

"We don't need this. You should stay."

Chase walked outside and disappeared in island darkness. I felt more frustrated now, and our best chance of finding Tatum Jones just left us, again. Kevin shrugged and turned away.

"What if he goes back to Diggs?" I asked and paced. "He doesn't have a car. Kevin, do you still have the key for Utopia?"

"I have the key. He won't leave this time. He's not that stupid."

"How can you be so sure?" I asked. "Since when do you have any faith in Chase?"

"He probably wants Diggs more than I want Tatum. He'll come back later tonight. I know he will."

"I'm going home," Dudas said. "But let's back up for a minute. Why's he talking about jail?"

"Butch is hiding money on Cayo Costa, and Miami PD was contacted by that banker's widow from New York. She's wanting the money her husband was hiding from her."

I was shocked at Kevin's honesty. Dudas had the same look Kevin had when he first found out about it. My necessary lie was out in the open now.

"But you said there wasn't any money," Dudas said with a look of confusion.

"I had to lie because I knew it would eventually come back to you and anyone else, I cared about. Hailey doesn't even know about it."

"How much?" Dudas asked.

"More than I feel comfortable telling you about."

"Hell, Chase took a hundred thousand of it," Kevin said. "He's in just as deep as you are."

Dudas poured a cup of steaming hot black coffee and took a sip. His eyes were still, and a familiar look of surprise showed in the chubby folds across his face.

"We can talk about this another time," Kevin said. "We need to go by the house."

"You can't go home," Dudas said. "I see police cruisers patrolling the complex every morning. They keep leaving notes for you on the front door. Hailey keeps calling too. I told her you had something to follow up on in Miami. You should call her today."

"Great—"

Someone knocked on the front door. I looked at Kevin, hoping it was Chase coming back. Dudas set the coffee down and walked toward the door.

"Hello, Dudas!" someone yelled from outside.

Dudas looked at me and motioned toward his office before half opening the door. A thin, middle-aged man with a receding hairline walked inside. He wore thick-framed glasses and walked with a cane.

"Your guy never showed up," the man said. "So, I thought I'd come to you."

"Now's not the best time," Dudas said.

I nodded at Kevin and walked toward the back door. This distraction was a good reason to leave and find Chase before he left us again. Kevin followed me outside.

"Where are you two going?" Dudas asked. "We aren't finished talking."

"We can't stay here anyway. Chief Diggs will eventually show up."

Dudas shook his melon-size head and went back to talking with the man. Kevin stopped near the glow of the porch light and lit a cigarette. The smell reminded me of dad. I stood in darkness and watched mangled banyan tree shoots move behind him.

* * *

North beach stretched out along a winding waterline with small waves that crested and rolled to the shoreline for only seconds before being pulled away. The stars above broke through scattered clouds that moved northeast. The calm wind cooled the sweat on my neck. I sat looking out at a blinking light from a skiff, miles offshore. My feet were buried in the cool sand, and I noticed there were no mosquitoes because of the wind.

My mind raced with thoughts of police corruption. I tried to remember looking up to police officers as a boy. They were real life superheroes then. I stood when the wind calmed down and walked out in the dark Gulf water to where the waves broke. The light from the far-off skiff still flashed on and off.

This beach reminded me of Hailey. It had been several days since missing my flight to Mexico and I wanted to hear her voice. My cell phone had been dead for days. Tarpon Marina was only a mile or so down shore. I could call her from there without wondering whether the phone was tapped.

The bright light from the lighthouse pushed out over the pass and incoming tide. I jogged away from Cayo Costa. It was a dark mass in the distance behind me. No boats. No lights. There were only the mangroves and hundreds of palm trees that gave the island substance. I turned inland and ran between sand dunes to where the path led up to the road toward Tarpon Marina.

The restaurant and bar were closed. I walked down the patio steps and grabbed the key under the back doormat. Once inside, I found a phone in the quiet kitchen and dialed the number Dudas had written down for me. The operator connected me to Hailey's room.

"Hello," a man answered the phone.

"Is Hailey there?" I asked.

"May I ask who's calling, please?"

"Butch."

The line went silent. I put the phone to my shoulder and turned to look behind me. Footsteps walked through the restaurant above me.

"You're okay, aren't you, son?" the man asked. "It's me, Conrad."

"I'm fine," I said. "Is Hailey okay?"

"She's good. Hold, please."

"Butch! Oh my god," Hailey sounded worried. "Are you okay?"

"I'm fine, Hailey. How was the—"

"Are you hurt? I can't believe you were shot. Dudas told me about the gas—"

"Trust me, Hailey, I'm fine. Tell me about the wedding. I'll explain everything when you fly home."

"But Dudas said the police were after you and that you were shot."

"My leg is fine. It wasn't a direct shot, just a ricochet. When did you talk to Dudas?"

"Two days ago. I'm sorry for being angry but I thought you just missed the flight. I had no idea that—"

"Hang on a second," I said and covered the phone to scan the kitchen.

A shuffling noise came from behind a line of sailboats outside the kitchen window. The shuffling stopped and the constant splashing noise from the live wells was all that remained.

"Do you know about Rose?" I asked still watching the sailboats.

"What about her?" Hailey asked.

"Listen. I need you to call Kevin—"

"Why do you keep covering the phone?"

"Hold on. I hear something."

"What about Rose?"

The shuffling was behind me now. Before I could turn to face it, a garbage bag came down over my head. A kick to the shin was followed by a jab to the side of my face. I struggled to reach around and grab for the one holding the bag but was swiftly put in a headlock and dropped hard to the pavement. It was hard to breathe.

"Butch! Are you there?" Hailey screamed through the dangling phone line.

Another punch followed and my ears rang. I stumbled back just before a deafening blow to my face. Flashes of light came with the stinging pain that pushed against the inside of my nose. I fell hard to the floor still gasping for air. Dark plastic stuck to my face and mouth. Breathing was impossible now. Seconds later, the sounds went away, and everything went black.

Chapter Eighteen

A constant pain pulsated between my swollen eyes and both shoulder blades were sore from the hard floor. I could not sleep in this rank, pitch-black room engulfed by humidity and damp heat. I tried to ignore an uncomfortable position and sat against a wall, sweating in silence for what seemed like three hours before a sudden obnoxious laughter grew outside the room. Two men laughed and spoke in broken English.

The door creaked open, and my dilated eyes winced at the bright yellow sunlight. One of them entered the room.

"You see him move, no?" the one outside asked.

"Think he's breathing," the other man said and pulled the door shut.

I was alone once again and used my hands to feel my way across the room before I knocked over a stack of crab traps. The smell of galvanized wire was strong and unpleasant.

Heavy feet suddenly hurried up steps from underneath the structure and the door opened again with the bright light filling the room. A tin plate was set at my feet and two bottles of something were placed beside me.

"Como esta, Butch? Rum, no?" the man said. "Your bread and oysters." He hurried out of the room.

I sat back on both hands and leaned against a crab trap. It was difficult to find the bottles of rum in the dark. I finally opened one of the bottles and enjoyed the sweet warm taste that filled my parched mouth just before a fire burned down my throat.

I grabbed one of the shucked oyster shells and quickly pinched the soft wet muscle from its place and set it on the end of my tongue before swallowing it whole. The dry bread was tasteless but helped with the rum burn. The oyster taste reminded me of something good. With each oyster, I ate faster until the plate was down to empty shells. A few of my fingertips bled with the sharp edges. I forced the bread down until the plate was empty. With a dry mouth, I took another long drink from the rum bottle and flinched at the long burn.

All sense of time had been lost since talking to Hailey on the phone at Tarpon Marina. I had no idea where I was now, and the question of who had done this to me ran nonstop through my mind. It had to be Tatum Jones. I clutched the bottle of rum and ran through possible scenarios.

* * *

I was awakened by the thud of someone hitting the stack of crab traps and falling to the ground next to me. A large man stood in the doorway, with sunlight shaping his massive silhouette.

"Next time, I'll kill you," he said and raised his arms. "Go

to hell," the man said and coughed.

"Not a sound," the large man said. "Either one of you moves, I'm back in here like that." The door slammed shut, taking all daylight with it.

"Who's that?" the man said in a familiar voice. "Butch Sands. Chase?"

"Bullshit," he said in a now familiar voice. "How did . . . when did they bring you out here?"

"Where's here?"

"Cayo Costa."

"Cayo Costa!"

"Is Kevin in here?"

"We were separated during an ambush at your house. Two days ago."

"It has been two days?"

"After I found a local doctor and got stitched up, I went back to the news building to find you. You were gone so I went to your house. Tatum's guy must have tracked me there."

"How did you lose Kevin?"

"Shot my way out and ran down the beach. I got one of them, but the other guy caught up with me near the lighthouse. Kevin's probably okay."

"Did you talk to Dudas?"

"No, he was meeting with someone. Left word with your secretary."

"Have you heard anything from your guys at Miami PD?"

"When you disappeared, I called my guy in Miami. He hadn't heard anything from Tatum in weeks, and Diggs has been up north in Jacksonville since last weekend. Everything's been relatively quiet."

Chase stood up and knocked over a crab trap. He stumbled into the door and fell back. I reached out to break his fall.

"Can't see a damn thing in here."

"Who brought you out here?"

Chase struck a match and the orange glow cast shadows along the far wall. The smell of cigarette smoke followed. I reached out for a cigarette. He lit a second before darkness fell again.

"Well," Chase said and exhaled. "Let's just say we've become top priority for Tatum Jones. That's what killing June Bug and shooting down one of his seaplanes got us." Laughter bellowed out. "I should've killed him down there. Two years with Miami PD never got me that close to him."

"What stopped you?"

"I want him to know why, just before it happens. Just me and him, alone. I want to hear him say her name before I blow his brains out."

"Kevin probably feels the same way."

"The night you disappeared, I borrowed a small flats boat and drove it through the pass. I figured Tatum might have had something to do with you disappearing, so I reacted on instinct."

"But where'd you—"

"I noticed some running lights and movement near the north end of the island. But I waited—"

Multiple gunshots rang out from the floor above our room. The door suddenly swung open, bringing sunlight back inside. An older Hispanic man shouted orders from the hallway.

"Get the pig out of here," the man said. "Put the other one in a chair and tie his hands behind him."

"I'm not leaving," Chase said and began to kick and swing wildly. He missed everything. "I'm Miami PD. You know that, right?"

"No choice," the bigger one said and bear-hugged Chase. "Hold the door."

"Get off me . . . Butch hold—"

"Hold him still, Julian."

The older man sucker-punched Chase and knocked him out. He yelled orders and walked around the commotion before kneeling to my level.

"Enough, B. Just take him down to the dock."

"They both did June Bug in . . . that's what Tatum said."

The man carried Chase out of the room. I noticed a half-smoked cigarette on the damp concrete floor.

"Don't say anything, Butch," Chase said before being thrown against the outside wall and punched again.

"Keep that damn light in here, B. Don't shut the door." The man pulled the cigarette from my mouth and grabbed me by the chin. He tilted it up before punching me hard across my good eye. My head snapped back. The man made a grunting sound and punched me again in the exact same place.

"Asshole journalist. Why'd you get involved?" he said and shoved me to the ground and wedged his knee across my chest. "We pay good money to stay anonymous. There must be ten or twelve bigger operations than ours, in Miami alone."

"I didn't ask to be shot at either," I said and spit blood in the man's face.

"Quiet," he said and grabbed me by the throat. I fought for air and could feel the circulation leaving my brain and my eyes began to water.

"I should kill you now," the man said before finally letting go of my throat.

I breathed hard until both lungs filled again. The man calmly pulled a vile from his shirt pocket. He opened it up and poured something on his index finger and snorted it.

"Where's Tatum?" I asked and started breathing easier now. "I need to see him."

The man picked up a small stack of crab-traps and used them for a doorstop. "Who's Tatum?"

"You tell me," I said and noticed the bloodied floor in the sunlight.

There was an abundance of dried crabs and fish carcasses. Tangled fishing nets filled the corners of the room, and long gaffs hung from hooks on all four walls. A few empty rum bottles littered the floor next to us.

"You work for the fat man on Pedro Island, right?" He poured more of the cocaine in the palm of his hand and snorted all of it.

"You know Dudas?"

"He never had the balls to expose us until now. Who knows how much he's benefited from this operation." He wiped the powder away from his nose and mouth and clumsily approached me. "What do you know?"

"About what—"

Another blow to the face knocked me over in the chair. The fall was worse than the punch. My face hurt everywhere.

"What made you think you could get away with killing June Bug?" He grabbed me by the shoulders.

"Self-defense." I ground my teeth in anticipation of another punch.

"Tell me, Butch Sands, where am I supposed to get a good cup of coffee when I'm down here?" He started laughing.

"What—"

He stopped laughing and quickly turned and kicked me flush in the face with a roundhouse. It happened too fast for a reaction. The blow to my head turned everything black and I fell to the floor.

Chapter Nineteen

A cool evening wind crept inside the foul-smelling room and made it bearable to breathe. I opened my eyes and rolled over to put my nose near the door and took in the salt and fresh air. There was no understanding of place and time. I was stiff and sore and hopeless.

With no warning, the door pushed open, and sunlight showed unfamiliar faces. They filed in one at a time and formed a semi-circle around me. Everyone in the room just stared in silence. The last one in the room left the door open.

"Chase is gone . . . and we're going to kill you," the oldest man said holding a sawed off 12-gauge shotgun.

I looked at everyone in the group around me. Each one was dressed in a filthy shirt and torn shorts, all barefoot and nappy. A well-dressed man walked in the room and stood near the open door. He looked out of place in a crowd of vulgar, modern-day vagabonds.

"So, our hero is finally awake," the well-dressed man said to the man holding the shotgun. "How much has he told the police?"

"Nada, Senior Tone," the man said, sounding confident. I looked over and recognized Tatum Jones through swollen eyes. I was unable to see his face until now. One of the younger looking men from the crowd set his machete down and grabbed me by the shoulders. I tightened my jaw.

"Tatum," I said. "Where've you been?"

"It has been a few days, right Butch?" Tatum said.

"Where's Chase?" I asked.

"Let's start with a very simple question," Tatum said and looked down at the gun. "How did you plan to kill me? I'm God down here, Butch. Think you can kill God?"

"Maybe," I said through bleeding gums.

"So, you come inside my home in the Keys. Walked into my kitchen while your brother hid in a closet strapped with guns and ammo? What were you looking for? Did you know the politician from the gas station? Asshole treated my people like animals." Tatum stood and moved the barrel of the gun close to my forehead. I looked at the nickel plate and teardrop tattoo. Sweat began to cool my neck and shoulders.

"Maybe I should shoot you in the face," Tatum said. "Maybe each shoulder to drag it out some." Tatum aimed the gun at my left shoulder and pulled the trigger.

Click.

"God!" I shouted.

"Empty," Tatum said and flipped open the chamber of the revolver and spun it. "One in six chances, Butch. Those odds aren't so bad." He pointed the gun at my other shoulder and smiled. "This might hurt."

"Okay . . . just don't—"

Click.

The small group laughed at my nervous behavior. Tatum turned and laughed with them. Every part of my face pulsated in pain. Hopelessness began to take hold of my psyche. This situation was hauntingly like the one I experienced about a month ago. Stranded and left to die on a remote Caribbean Island, pursued by pirates looking for promised money. The irony now is that the same money is buried about two hundred yards from this very place. But they have no idea about the money. Tatum Jones spends more in a month than I have buried.

"Let's try again, Butch," Tatum said and stopped laughing. He turned and pointed the gun at my forehead. "How do you know Chase Anderson?"

The question seemed as odd as the situation. His narrow eyes looked straight into mine. I could smell the cigar smoke in his facial hair. He leaned in, uncomfortably close.

"Why didn't you ask me this in New Orleans? You act like this is the first time we've met. We spent an hour together?"

"Answer the question." Tatum shrugged.

I wasted no time answering. "He tried to arrest me."

"Go on," Tatum said, holding still as a statue.

"He was assigned my case by Chief Diggs at Miami PD," I said with an obvious sensibility in my voice. "Your guy, right?"

"What the hell does that mean?" Tatum asked. "Politicians, Chiefs of police, rookie cops . . . they all work for me. I own everyone down here."

The crowd was less jovial than before, and a new energy filled the room. I prayed that someone would walk in and stop this before it ended badly. Chase was my only hope at this point.

"Why chase me across Florida to New Orleans with a rookie, nobody cop? Do you want something from me? Money? Women? Drugs?"

"Revenge."

"For what?" Tatum kept the barrel close.

"The girl at the gas station."

"What girl?"

There was a short pause. I watched his eyes change with the realization of who the girl was. Tatum pulled the barrel of the gun away. He shrugged again.

"She wasn't the target. Who was she to you? No woman is worth dying for."

I wanted to tackle him against the wall. He could care less about Rose or my brother's lost life. They were not on his payroll. Neither one moved the meter for his enterprise. Everyone was a commodity.

"You know, I've protected Chase Anderson for two years now," Tatum said as he removed his sport-coat. "And now, he just decides to help a journalist out on some crazy revenge trip. You're a journalist, right?"

"Yes."

"What lies did Chase tell you about me?"

"He won't say much about anything. All I know to this point is that you run some kind of smuggling operation out of Miami. And you have a history with him."

"Very good. He reached in the pocket of freshly pressed pants and pulled out my wallet and read from the driver's license. "Is this a current address?"

"Why?"

"Who else do you know that would talk? Your fiancée, Hailey Thomas, she comes from money, right?"

"She's been out of town—"

"In Mexico, I know. You should've boarded that flight."

"Who told you that?"

"You know, Butch, there's a difference between taxable and slush money. Chief Diggs happens to fall in the latter. All he ever did was collect money and shut his mouth. Like a puppet on strings, you know? Kind of similar to that fat bearded puppet you work for at the Island Courier."

"Why are you holding me here?"

"Remember something, Butch, you're not interviewing me," Tatum said standing now with arms crossed. "I'm going to kill you either way.

Chase will find out the hard way, so just cooperate with the questions and it'll all be over soon enough."

"I'm done talking—"

"One in six, Butch," Tatum said and pointed the gun at my shoulder again and pulled the trigger.

Click.

"Asshole!"

"Let's go again," Tatum said but aimed the gun at my head this time.

"Wait! All right . . . let's finish this . . . ask me anything you want." I turned away from the gun. "Just put the gun down and I'll talk."

"Excellent choice," Tatum said and opened the chamber. He emptied the single bullet in my lap. "Catch." I held the bullet and closed swollen eyes. Darkness filled my thoughts. Hope was a glimmer of light filtering through cracks in the surrounding walls.

"Now, what have you sent to your newspaper? Tell me what the fat man knows."

"Nothing. Dudas hasn't had a chance to pressure me for a story yet."

"Everyone out!" Tatum said and motioned for everyone to leave. *"Vamanos!"*

He paced back and forth before stopping to pick up one of the freshly painted crab traps from the far corner of the room. He held it up to look at the entry door with the bent wire for the crab to enter the food chamber. The narrow passage and bend of the wire would inevitably keep the crab from ever escaping.

"Do you feel trapped, Butch?" Tatum asked in a muffled voice. "Hopeless, maybe?"

"No."

"How can you say that? You're obviously here against your will."

"Things turn out the way they're supposed to, I guess."

"True. Now that I think about it, you really had no way of avoiding that gas station shootout, or your first encounter with Chase Anderson. And the rest of it would've inevitably followed."

"What are you talking about?"

He pulled a thin tin box from his pants pocket and opened it. He grabbed a neatly rolled joint and held it up to a lighter and lit it. The orange flame cast his long shadow along the far wall. I watched it smoke and could smell the marijuana.

"You smoke? Take a hit."

"Why am I here?"

"You know the answer to that," Tatum said and pulled an enormous money-roll out of his other pocket and dangled it in my face. "See this . . . a roll of fifty grand makes you feel powerful."

"I won't write a story."

"It's irrelevant. New information is meaningless for you at this point."

He stuffed the money-roll back in his pocket and went back to smoking marijuana. I was tired of talking and my head was throbbing now.

"I don't understand how I pose such a threat."

"I felt the same way . . . until you killed June Bug and ran to New Orleans looking for me," he said and held the next hit in before smoke streamed out from his nose. "You should've left it alone." He coughed hard for about ten seconds.

"I have no story . . . to this point."

"No reason to lie."

He followed the coughing spell with another hit. I tried to think of the right things to say. But for some reason, my thoughts went back to a volunteer counseling job I had before college. Talking to Tatum reminded me of unsuccessful counseling sessions I had with Big Ruben, the Alpha Male at the Northern Kentucky halfway house that employed me part time out of college. I never could relate to his situation or past. I remember Big Ruben's only soft side was the baby daughter he'd never seen. How his daughter was the only reason he had to live. The only reason he'd ever sold cocaine in the first place.

"Stay with me," Tatum said through a cloud of smoke.

"Is this a way to reach out to your father? You never had one, right?"

"Who . . . what are you talking about?" He gently placed the butt of the joint on the floor and watched it burn out completely. "What's that have to do with your situation?"

"He abandoned you, right?"

"No . . . but what does that have to do with you?"

"What's your full name?"

"This is pointless. I don't know why I listened to him in the first place."

"Who?" I asked knowing this topic pressed hard on his nerves. "Who's him?"

Tatum rubbed his chin with a cold look of frustration. Irritation and fatigue began to change him. I knew he was frustrated about holding a person captive. It must be cumbersome for him. Kilos could not speak. Cocaine had no voice or care. Money could be washed. But talking to a journalist must be the worst situation, especially for a spoon-fed drug dealer who seemed to have never taken a punch in his life.

"Information won't do you any good. Just enjoy your permanent vacation. The fat man, Dudas, will get by without you. He always has." He checked his gold watch and smiled. "Maybe Hailey flew in early from the wedding. Maybe she's at your place right now. Maybe I could give her what you never could."

His mood changed again, and he danced around me with fists raised. I followed his eyes for a moment before he unloaded a jab hook combination that knocked me to the ground. I rolled over in pain and felt for my front teeth. The room spun and my energy slowly slipped away.

Chapter Twenty

A voice barely above a whisper came from the next room over. I had trouble hearing what was being said and ignored it for a time while concentrating solely on eating the last three oysters. My newfound numbness for smell and taste made the once delightful oyster seem more of a thick rubber band dipped in warm sweat. I tossed the muscle into my dry mouth and leaned down near the corner of the room where a slight crack allowed the dimmest of light to pass through. The voice continued.

"Butch," the raspy voice said.

"Who's there?"

"Chase."

I was surprised to hear his voice and felt hopeful for the first time in days. Thought he was dead. The crack in the floorboard provided a clear channel for conversation. I leaned down to put my ear against it. The smell was getting worse by the day.

"How are you holding up, Butch?"

"Hungry . . . tired."

Our conversation was suddenly interrupted by footsteps overhead. I scratched the scruff on my chin and neck and waited in silence. The back-and-forth walking continued for several minutes until the sound from an opening door eventually faded.

"Chief Diggs found me on the North beach. He asked about you, and what our motives were, chasing after Tatum."

"Where'd they question you?"

"Your office. Tatum waited at your desk looking through a pile of pictures. Paperwork had been thrown everywhere, and your computer files were printing off the entire time we were there."

"Where was Dudas?"

I feared that Dudas was somehow involved in this. Especially after hearing about the hush money, he'd received from Tatum Jones over the past few years.

"It was just Tatum and a few others. No one else was there."

"What about local police? They're looking for us, right?"

"Not as much. Tatum told me he'd paid out cash to a few sheriffs on our behalf. He said it was more than two months' salary for them."

"What about Diggs?"

"My guy in Miami, Peterson, had nothing new to say when we talked yesterday."

"Peterson?"

"Yeah. He's one of our narc guys."

"Good to know his name."

"Yeah. If you ever need something, just let Peterson know you know me."

"What about Kevin?"

"The night you disappeared; I went by your place. Kevin's things were still there but he was gone. I left a note on the kitchen counter for you to call me."

"Where was he?"

"I'm not sure. He's probably wondering where you are at this point. And who knows if Hailey has called the police from Mexico."

"We need to escape, Chase. Tatum will kill me. I'm not staying here another night. You can only stand to smell your own piss and body odor for so long."

"I know. I'll think of something here soon—"

"I don't even care about writing a story, that's the funny thing about this whole situation. I did at first, you know, but now, it just doesn't seem worth the risk. I'd rather watch Tatum Jones go to prison than write a feature about his life of corruption."

"I still want to kill him."

"I don't. Not the way Kevin wants to."

"You should always avoid killing anyone, at all costs."

"What are you talking about? I watched you blow June Bug's brains out the back of his head. What was that?"

"I never said that I hadn't done it. That's part of my job description. I kill the bad guys to protect the innocent. You know, most murders are never even covered by news reporters."

"Who was your first?"

"My stepdad. Shot the bastard when I was twelve," Chase said. "One day, I decided to end the beatings he gave me and my mom." Deep breathing followed. "He's the reason I played baseball every day of my youth. Every batter I faced . . . was *him*. Threw inside fastballs mostly. Had a reputation of being fearless. Never intentionally walked anyone."

"Look, I don't need to—"

"It's all right. I need to talk about it occasionally to people I trust."

I was surprised to hear the word trust. Chase Anderson was a complicated person to know, but the longer I knew him, the more I understood why.

"He finished with mom, you know, she'd stopped screaming for a couple minutes before I heard him walking down the hallway toward my room. He was a trial lawyer with money, and the house was big with long hallways," Chase had a sick laugh between sentences. "So, I loaded the revolver a friend stole for me, and I pretended like I was sleeping." A long pause came next. Chase passively cleared his throat then laughed again. "You wouldn't happen to have a cigarette, would you?"

"No," I said, anticipating what happened next.

"You couldn't hand it to me anyway," Chase said and cleared his throat again. "I missed with the first shot but got him in the right shoulder with the next one. He screamed and fell to a knee. Then, when he turned to see if she was coming, I shot him in the head . . . and he fell to the floor. Mom came into the room, crying hysterically."

"What'd she do?"

"She started hugging him and talking to him. I got out from under the covers and put on some warmer clothes. It was freezing outside."

"You left?"

"I walked out the front door."

"Seriously?"

"Two days later, I found a homeless shelter. They called child services and put me in a foster home. I never told them where I'd come from."

"So, you never got caught?"

"No. I haven't seen my mom since then either."

"Where's home?"

"Atlanta."

"Sorry about that. Couldn't imagine a bully for a father."

"You were lucky. Even my real dad left when I was five."

"Damn."

"It is what it is, you know."

"I guess."

"Get some rest. Don't think about these guys right now. When they come for us . . . just be ready."

"I'm sick of this whole thing."

"Look, you're involved now, regardless of desire or merit. Your writing can help fight my cause. You've seen too much. There's no way you can ignore it at this point. You're in it, Butch."

"But—"

"The next time they come for you, be ready."

"For what?"

"I have a gun—"

"A gun . . . how do you still have a gun?"

"Just be ready."

I leaned back away from the crack in the floor and felt somewhat guilty for wanting to give up, but that opportunity ceased to exist because giving up meant dying. I trusted that Chase could get me out, especially now, after hearing his story. He is a survivor. Always has been.

"You know they're after Tatum, right?" Chase continued to talk.

"Miami PD."

"But aren't they together in all of this?"

"They never really liked each other, June Bug kind of played mediator between them. Most of Tatum's family lives in low-income housing projects in Miami owned by that politician he killed at the gas station shooting."

"Did he evict Tatum's cousin or something?"

"No. Last month, he had one of his landlords evict everybody, Tatum's brothers, uncles, nephews, and children. All of them."

"Did you know about this the whole time?"

"Yes."

"You knew why Tatum shot up the gas station and didn't tell me?"

"Yeah. What would that have changed?"

"And you knew why he did it, too?"

"Why would I tell you? You were not involved then."

"True. But I was involved when you shot June Bug, and what about New Orleans. Why didn't you tell me then? I probably could have avoided this if—"

"If what? Who were you going to run and tell? You were better off not knowing."

"That's bullshit and you know it," I said and leaned back out of listening range until Chase's voice finally went silent.

I was angry for not knowing about Tatum's situation with the politician. Part of me understood why Chase kept it a secret, but that didn't make it right. To understand why it had happened wasn't getting me out of this place alive. Nor was it doing me any good now. I toiled with the idea of yelling for anyone to come down and finish off this misery for good. These guys could be provoked. But I could not get myself to yell. All I could think about was Hailey.

I listened to the incoming tide outside. It brushed up against the shoreline below the room. The thought of seeing her again gave me something to hold onto for now. She gave me hope. She kept me alive.

Chapter Twenty-One

The soft shuffling sound from hundreds of hermit crabs filtered through the cracks in the floor. I lay outstretched with my left ear over the widest crack in the floor; my nose was nearly touching the corner of the warped wall. My aching body made it difficult to sleep for most of last night. The shuffling below came and went with the incoming tide. I envisioned hundreds of them searching for higher ground beneath the mangroves outside.

I sat up, away from the avenue of fresh air, and flinched at the stout smell of galvanized wire that had strengthened in recent days. I was boxed into the far corner of the room, surrounded by the freshly made crab traps along with mangled and used ones harboring dried fish skeletons and dead blue crabs. The crab traps had been tossed inside the room ten to twenty at a time throughout the night. I had formed a blockade with the old ones to avoid being hit when more were thrown in.

Chase had been quiet for several hours and no one had harassed either of us since the last interrogation session involving Tatum and a machete. The raw oysters still came every six to seven hours, sometimes with more rum and stale bread.

The hope of ever seeing Hailey or anyone else was beginning to fade. My built-up anger from the countless hours being held against my will had changed from sadness, to hopelessness, to carelessness, and now, faithlessness.

I thought about the same Kentucky inmate, named Ruben Daily. The other inmates called him Big Ruben for obvious reasons. Big Ruben had always referred to being locked up as institutionalism. He would say that parole wasn't enough to shake it, how being locked up like an animal would change anybody... regardless of their beliefs. He'd go on explaining how every one of us would deal with institutionalism at some point in our lives, whether it was marriage, career, cocaine, sex, or even money. The vice was irrelevant, he'd say. Everybody but Jesus, he would proclaim. In his eyes, there was no escape, not even for the ones smart enough to trick themselves with religion. Some could, he would chuckle, but ninety-nine percent were locked up in their own minds for a life sentence. A few of his closest friends, according to him, were born with a life sentence.

I rolled away from the pile of crab traps and ground my teeth in anger. Fearlessness came again, followed by a sudden jolt of sadness. Another lost hour passed before footsteps sounded up on the floor above. They ran across the room and barreled down steps before stopping. The door kicked open, and a flashlight shined in my face.

"You awake in here?"

I covered both dilated eyes and lay still on the floor hoping they would leave a dead man alone. Two men made their way through piles of crab traps. I stayed still and hoped they would not get to my corner. But they did, eventually.

"Stand up!" The one holding the flashlight yelled.

I ignored the order and stayed motionless on the floor. There was no reason to cooperate now. Cooperation had done nothing for me to this point.

"It's an improvement, don't you think, Julian?" One of them knelt and examined my bruised face with the flashlight.

"No. He's almost as skinny as you now, B." the man said and pulled at my shirt, lifting me off the floor.

The other one called B, grabbed me under both armpits and pulled me to my feet. They turned me sideways and both grabbed an arm.

"Damn, that smell is something fierce."

"Just start walking with him."

Chasing Palms

I let both feet drag while they walked me around crab traps, then outside of the dingy room. The hallway was dark and narrow. I caught glimpses of the two with the shaking flashlight. Neither one of their faces was clear enough to see. They hurried me up steps through blurry darkness. Julian was much taller than his counterpart. His dreadlocks fell around broad shoulders. He carried most of the weight. B was the weaker of the two. He smelled of incense and marijuana. His thick beard and bushy hair brushed up against the side of my neck, every step itching me.

"White boy has definitely lost some weight."

"Yeah, what, about six pounds you think?"

"Too bad he couldn't have let it alone, you know. Tone is still pissed."

"You want to be a hero, huh Butch? You should've known when to stop looking. This could be the end of it though. You went too far."

My mindset went back to hopelessness. There was nothing to say, especially to these two. Listening and not responding was the best response to their instigative and probing remarks.

"You had it good, man. Not sure what ratting us out proves. But that's what you do, isn't it? You're just a rat journalist," B said and started laughing.

"No more talking, B."

"Who cares about us, Jules? Hell, we're stress relief."

"Shut up! You know we're not supposed to talk to him," Julian stopped walking just before we reached the top.

"Who the fu—"

"Watch it, B. I'll drop him and kick your ass quick."

"We'll see about that."

"Just quit talking."

"Fine."

We continued up to the rooftop. The surrounding seascape was black. No moon. No lighthouse. There was only the clean crisp Gulf breeze that moved the surrounding palm trees. The air was the cleanest I had breathed for days.

"Get the other one," a man said, walking toward us.

I recognized the man's voice and watched him light a cigarette. The fire from the tip glowed then brightened when he inhaled. The smell of smoke was sweet and inviting to my warped senses.

"Where do you want this one?" Julian asked.

"Help him find a seat," the man said and inhaled again. A pause preceded two quick punches to my gut. In my weakened state, the blows dropped me instantly. I struggled to push up from the rooftop before being kicked square in the rib section. My face planted firmly on the dried wooden surface.

"That's enough," the man said, standing over me.

"Let's get the other one," B said and lit a joint before he walked back down the narrow steps. "Telling you, Tone, we need to let these fools shower or something."

"Shut up," Julian said as they went down the steps. "Thought we could wrap this interview up, finally?"

"Having a pleasant stay, I presume," Tatum said and tossed the glowing cigarette over the edge of the roof.

"Sure."

"My business model doesn't usually involve human cargo. I can push any product, but they don't usually talk," Tatum lit another cigarette and approached me. "How much have you told the fat man, in regard to my operation?"

"Everything . . . I told him everything."

"You couldn't have known everything before we kidnapped you."

"Good journalism . . . I guess."

"What about—"

The banging sound from someone being pushed up against a wall interrupted our conversation. A silent pause preceded the click and pull of a gun chamber being loaded. Tatum Jones turned his head toward the empty stairway. When no one appeared, he went back to questioning me.

"I don't need you. Everyone else was easy. All they needed was money. It was simple to make them look the other way. Hell, I give two hundred thousand dollars a year in donations to keep Cayo Costa an environmentally sound wildlife sanctuary. Did your research expose that fact?"

"It's too late. The story's been leaked. I mailed a package to the Associated Press and the FBI the morning we came back from New Orleans. Someone should be watching your house in the Keys as we speak."

"Dudas would have told me that by now. You're bluffing."

"If that helps you."

"You'll be dead—"

Gunshots fired below the deck. Tatum jumped over me and ran toward the steps. A struggle ensued, followed by the sounds of fists connecting to flesh. Desperation grunts followed.

Three more shots were fired. A few seconds of silence followed. Someone ran up the steps.

"Butch!" Chase yelled out.

A sixth shot fired, and the sound of Chase's voice was silenced. I walked toward the stairway. A lone figure stood at the bottom step.

"I've got Tatum. Jump off and swim! Forget about—" Two quick gunshots from a smaller gun silenced Chase.

I felt a rush of adrenaline and hurried along the declining slope to where it dropped off. The edge overlooked dark churning water.

"Butch," Tatum struggled to speak.

I fought for balance and looked out across the dark pass, searching for the usually dependent beam of light from the lighthouse. But nothing came. Dark, hammerhead infested water moved twenty feet below.

"The lighthouse isn't—"

Chase's voice went silent, and I froze at the idea of swimming against an overpowering tide. Heavy footsteps scampered up the stairwell. Fear changed my brief cautious thinking. I expected another gunshot just before jumping. But nothing came.

The fall twisted my stomach up until I slammed belly first into saltwater. Bubbles filled the cold wet darkness that instantly surrounded me. I kicked and paddled with everything I had left. The beach was farther away than I anticipated it being. Nearly a full minute went by before my burning nose and aching mouth reached the surface. I gasped for oxygen, continuing to move every extremity as fast and hard as I could stand.

I swam away from a sudden beam of light and the forceful current pulled me outward and rolled me under. I gave way to the untamable force and could no longer swim against it. A cold feeling tightened in my aching chest. I closed my eyes with the stinging saltwater and accepted the dark and tranquil water as fate.

Chapter Twenty-Two

Wet darkness cooled my aching body. I coughed continuously, working phlegm and saltwater out of my throat and lungs. A hand lifted my chin up and another hand rolled me over to prevent more choking. Mosquitoes buzzed in my ears and made an uncomfortable situation worse.

"You're going to make it, Butch. Get it out. That's it, keep coughing it up," Kevin's voice resonated in my mind. "You're alive."

"Kevin . . . when did you?"

I let my head fall to the side and waited for the coughing to stop. Wet sand pressed against my shoulders and my legs were still under water. The breathing finally eased back to normal.

"We've got you now. I don't know how."

"Yeah. Everything's fine, son," a husky voice came from a short distance away.

"Do you see anyone, Dudas?" Kevin asked and held my head out of the sand.

"No. No one followed us . . . luckily."

"We need to get him inside somewhere, Kevin. Get him some food and water."

"Where's Chase?" I asked. "He's still back there."

"Relax, Butch. We've got you now," Kevin said in a soft voice.

"Where'd you come from, Kevin? I should've drowned."

"Save your energy." Kevin held onto me.

"How'd you know I was out there?" I asked and tried to walk before falling to my knees. "The current was too strong, I couldn't—"

"You're fine now, Butch," Dudas said looking down at me. "We'll get you some food and a bed. What time is it, Kevin?"

"One thirty, I think," Kevin said and checked his watch. "Quarter till two."

"Joe's probably closing Marker 17 down as we speak."

I let go of Kevin and found a place to sit alone in the sand. My breathing was finally normal, and the fight of my life had exhausted my body.

"You think we should carry him that far?" Kevin asked. "We'll take the boat around the island and tie off to something near the public beach. Once we get him up there, I'll take the boat back to Tarpon Marina."

"Yeah, we shouldn't chance it," Dudas said, hovering now.

They helped me walk along the shoreline to where Kevin's boat was tied off to a gumbo-limbo tree. They lifted my torso over the bow and sat me in one of the fighting chairs. Dudas clumsily rolled aboard in front of me.

"Hold yourself up, Butch," Kevin said. "We need to push her off the sand bar."

"I'll get out and push her myself," Dudas said and rolled overboard into the shallows.

"Fine. Hang on, Butch." Kevin hurried up along the deck.

The three hundred horse outboard engines came to life with the muffle sound from stainless-steel propellers. Kevin tilted the trim and forced the propellers down until water churned off the stern.

"That's far enough. Swim around." Kevin killed the engine in the deeper water before he hurried back to help.

"That's it. Get me up there," Dudas said straining to climb aboard.

Kevin pulled him over the railing and went back to the captain's chair. Dudas sat hunched over next to me. He breathed heavily for almost a minute, then sat upright and gave me a pat on the back before joining Kevin near the controls.

I watched the blurred darkness slide by with the humming sound from the engines. The blowing wind and rough water brought me out of an energy slump. I watched Dudas and Kevin standing there, shirts and hair flailing in the wind, and felt thankful they saved my life. I just hoped Chase made it out alive.

* * *

Kevin tilted the trim up and killed the engines just before sliding the hull onto a vacant beach. I sat watching the big Gulf waters behind us. The overcast had no moon. Water and sky mended together to make charcoal blue with bits of whitecaps dotting the seascape.

"Luckily, there's no sand bar along this stretch," Kevin said as he walked along the railing.

"Yeah, this was our best chance with the tide," Dudas said and stood to stretch his enormous frame.

"Find us something to tie off from," Kevin said and tossed the mooring lines.

"There should be a pine-tree or something," Dudas said and hopped over the starboard side and jogged up the beach.

Kevin walked back to the bow and sat in the other fighting chair next to me. He leaned back and lit a cigarette. The smell of smoke carried on the breeze pushing inland.

"Chase is dead," I said. "He saved my life."

There was a long pause. The orange glow from the cigarette dimmed some. Kevin was in deep thought about something. It brightened again and he sat up.

"Who killed him?"

"I don't know. He screamed and then I jumped. They were shooting at me."

"You didn't have a choice. I would have jumped, too," Kevin put an arm around me.

"But how did you know where I was?" I asked.

"Dudas and I patrolled the pass for a few straight nights. We didn't trust the police or Coast Guard. Too much corruption tied to Tatum Jones and Chief Diggs. We heard gunshots and went in that direction. Must have gone by that old fish house ten times in two days. Can't believe you were in there."

"Why's Dudas with us?" I asked, remembering what Tatum said about paying him off too. "He's in Tatum's pocket. Always has been."

"No way," Kevin said with a look of surprise.

"I know it doesn't sound right, but Dudas works for them, too. Tatum told me."

"You're not making sense, Butch. All I'm concerned about is your health at this point. Besides, Dudas insisted we stay out longer than we planned. He's the reason we found you."

"I don't doubt that. But he's been taking money from the same guy who killed Grace and Rose."

An uncomfortable silence came next. The pleasant Gulf wind filled the spaces between words until Dudas finally came up to the boat. His breathing was raspy and uneasy.

"She's tied off securely," Dudas said. "Let's get him up there so I can move her."

"Look, try not to think right now," Kevin said with an arm around my aching shoulders. "We're taking you to Marker 17 for food and rest."

I felt my stomach growl. My throat was scratchy, and my muscles still ached from swimming in the pass. Everything had happened so fast since jumping.

"I'm fine with that."

"Let us help you, Sands," Dudas said and reached over the side to help me out of the boat.

"I can walk on my own," I said and pulled away.

"Stubborn as usual." Dudas threw up his arms in frustration. "Make sure we get everything, Kevin."

"All I have is one backpack," Kevin said and walked the deck. "I'll hose her off at the marina. Let's walk him up there together. Hopefully, no one followed us."

Kevin helped me keep my balance as he stepped over the railing. I had regained some strength and pushed away from the two and walked on my own through the dark landscape. The strain in my wounded leg came with each step but the sand was cool and dry just before we reached the steps that led up to the street. Kevin and Dudas followed close behind. No one spoke another word until we reached the top.

"Look out for patrol cars, Sands," Dudas said. "They're still looking for the three of you."

"Wouldn't I want them to find me, at this point?" I asked, surveying the dark street. "Unless Chief Diggs got to our local PD."

"No. Your case is still open with Miami PD. Probably a warrant out for your arrest, too."

Headlights along Palm Avenue stopped the conversation. I ducked behind a cluster of coconut palms and waited for the car to pass. It was a station wagon with Wisconsin plates. After the car passed, I limped across the shell filled street toward the awning of Marker 17 Tavern.

"Tatum Jones owns Miami PD and most of the decision makers along the Gulf Coast," I said looking at Dudas. "Including the media."

"You can't be serious. How could Tatum Jones be that powerful?" Dudas sounded out of breath from walking.

"He runs everything. But you already know that," I said and stopped at the front door of Marker 17 Tavern. "How much you get annually, Dudas?"

Kevin said, "Let me take a look inside first." He walked around us to open the front door. "Stay right here."

"How would . . . what are you talking about, Sands?" Even in the dim light, I could see that Dudas' cheeks were red.

"You've taken hush money for years."

"Sands!" Dudas shouted.

Kevin stuck his head out and nodded. His eyes scanned the street twice. I followed him inside.

"Go ahead, Butch. I see Joe counting money at the bar," Kevin said and looked over his shoulder.

"I'll see you later, Kevin. Thanks, Joe," Dudas said and slammed the front door shut. He was gone.

I followed Kevin across the dark bar. The air conditioning gave the room a coolness that was inviting. Joe the bartender looked up from a stack of money on the familiar oak bar and nodded at me. I felt hopeful for the first time in days.

Chapter Twenty-Three

A lone kitchen light ran along the floorboards toward the bar. Joe sat on a barstool directly across from where I drank my third bottle of beer. He shook his head in disbelief at what I was saying about my captors. Kevin sat next to him, urging me to eat more conch fritters and fried clams.

"So, Tatum Jones controls everyone?" Joe asked. "All of Miami PD, too?"

"It's not that simple," I said. "It's like a corporation."

"You've been gone for four days," Kevin said after pouring a shot of bourbon. "Look at your damn face. Still can't believe you survived."

"It felt longer than that," I said and squeezed lime juice on a conch fritter. "Days blended together."

"That sonuvabitch has been coming in here for ten years, and the whole time I was catering to a drug dealer," Joe said, noticeably aggravated.

"He's stayed private for a long time," I said and chased the sweet fried taste with beer. "I guess no cop ever challenged him before. Chase must've been the first."

Dudas pushed the front door open and hurried inside. He approached the bar sweating profusely. Kevin got up from his barstool to make room. I stayed focused on the food.

"That was fast. Anyone at the marina?" Kevin asked and walked over to a window and looked outside.

"No. The docks were clear," Dudas said and motioned for Joe to get him a drink.

"What did they feed you out there, Butch? You're thin as a rail," Joe said as he mixed a rum and diet.

"Raw oysters with stale bread and rum."

"How often did they feed you?" Dudas asked as he watched Joe mix his drink. "Sounds awful."

"They'd put a dozen on a plate every five to six hours. After a few days of that, your body starts rejecting them. The rum really saved me."

I took another drink of beer and tried to remember everything that had happened. I wanted to write the story now but could only think about food and resting first.

Dudas kept on with the questions. "How'd you manage to escape like you did?"

"You'll have to read about it," I said and smiled for the first time in days.

"What about Chase? Any chance he's still alive?"

"No chance," I said and paused to clear my throat.

I remembered hearing his voice just before jumping. A part of me thinks he's still alive. But telling Dudas this possibility did nothing good for anyone in his situation. If he's alive, he'll find us. There was no doubt in my mind.

"You think we need to help him—"

"That's insane, Kevin. We should call the FBI right now. Let them clean up that mess out there—"

"What happened to it being our problem to fix? Besides, who's going to believe us? Tatum Jones probably has them in his pocket, too."

"He's right, Dudas. We need to go back and see if he's alive," Kevin said. He lit a cigarette before sliding the pack down the bar to me.

Dudas laughed at the idea. "I'm not going out there without an arsenal of cops."

"Isn't there a cop Chase knows that you can trust?" Joe asked and pulled his own pack of cigarettes out from behind the bar and lit one.

"Yeah, did he give you a name or anything?" Dudas kept on with the questions.

"All Tatum Jones told me about was the hush money," I said and glared at Dudas. "Does hush money mean anything to you?" I watched the sweat bead off Dudas' melon sized forehead.

"That's absurd, Sands. They've offered it more than once, but how could I live with that on my conscience? You have to believe that I never accepted it. Hell, your father was offered more than you could imagine over the years," Dudas said but stopped talking during an uncomfortable pause. "He didn't take it either. No one with any dignity would take it."

"You shouldn't believe him," Kevin said and blew a smoke ring over the bar. "They could've told you anything out there."

"So, Tatum Jones's involvement isn't new to you then?" I asked, irritated with Dudas.

"Remember who you work for, Sands. You shouldn't believe everything you hear," Dudas said and stood from the bar.

"It sounded—"

"No. That's enough for tonight. Get your rest and I'll see you in the morning," Dudas said and walked across the dark dining area and picked a pool cue up from the table.

"I really need to call Hailey," I said to Joe.

"Use the room in the back. There's a shower and a phone," Joe said and pulled a key from below the bar and handed it to me. "Sleep for a while. I'll make sure no one knows you're back there."

"Yeah, get cleaned up and get some rest," Kevin said and patted me on the back. "We'll worry about all of this tomorrow."

I stood from the bar stool and ached all over. Lack of good sleep had finally caught up with me. I turned and noticed Dudas staring at me. His look was grave and untrusting.

"You should get out of town for a while," Dudas said and shook his head. "There's nothing you can change over-night."

I looked at Kevin. "I'm not running from this. We're not running from this. I need to see him, dead or alive, to put this behind me . . . behind us."

"They must have put a hurting on you with your face bruised like that," Joe said. He scooped some ice from the beer cooler and put it in a plastic bag for me.

"Thanks, Joe," I said and placed the cold ice over my swollen eye. "You should get on a plane and see Hailey. Forget about this for a while," Dudas said.

"You're probably right, but I can't ignore this. They were going to kill me out there. I can't just forget about that. They killed Rose too, remember," I said, looking directly at Kevin.

Headlights shone through the front windows. Joe walked around the bar to look out at the parking lot. I froze in anticipation.

"Get back there, Butch. Someone's here," Joe said and hurried for the front door.

"We'll both stay here tonight," Kevin said and motioned for me to get out of sight.

"I'm glad you're alive, Sands," Dudas said and ignored the visitor. His mood turned sullen, and he went back to his drink. "Go on, we'll manage this."

I turned around and walked toward an open door at the end of a narrow hallway. Strange voices came from the front foyer. Joe spoke up and turned them away in a hurry. The back room was cooler than the barroom, and the sheets on the bed were clean. I laid back across the bed and took in a deep breath, and then picked up the phone to call Hailey. Kevin stood in silence in the back hallway, waiting for anything to happen but it never did.

Chapter Twenty-Four

I rolled out of bed at sunrise and noticed clean clothes and a note on the bamboo dresser across the small room. My bruised face still hurt and swollen eyes barely opened. The dim sunlight showed Kevin's words. He asked to meet him around eight a.m. at Tarpon Marina. I looked at my messy hair and facial hair in a small bathroom mirror. My beard was longer than I can ever remember.

Joe was sleeping with his head on the bar as I crept through the empty room. No sign of Kevin or Dudas as I walked out the front door. An early morning thunderstorm was breaking up with pockets of rain still falling over Palm Avenue. I noticed Dudas drinking coffee under a blue awning across the street.

"Are you rested, Sands?" Dudas asked as a golf cart passed between us. "Thought you might sleep longer."

"What are you doing out here?"

"We've got some work to do," Dudas said as he crossed the street and walked past me toward the *Island Courier* building.

"Who was that last night?" I asked, and reluctantly followed. "Who showed up?"

"Chief Diggs."

"Are you serious?"

"He was drunk."

"What did he say?"

"He had some younger woman with him. They just wanted a place to sit and drink. He never mentioned you or Chase or anything."

"Does he know—"

"Joe handled it well. He gave them directions to some bar on the mainland."

"I need to call Peterson."

"Who's Peterson?"

"Forget about Peterson. Let's get out of the street," I said and jogged ahead of Dudas. "Is the door unlocked?"

"Think I left it open last night."

Inside, the newsroom was a disaster. Someone had ransacked the entire office. Tables were turned over and file cabinets lay empty on the floor. Even the kitchen area had been worked over. Dudas walked in behind me, frantic.

"What in the hell—"

"They're looking for a copy of the story," I said and hurried to my desk. "But I haven't written it yet."

"Find a phone, Sands. No time to clean this mess," Dudas said, walking over piles of paperwork.

"You should at least report this to someone," I said and cleared my desk of photographs and papers. "Tatum must be alive. No one else would do this."

"Who can I trust to call?" Dudas asked and picked up the phone.

"Dial Miami PD."

"No way—"

"Just dial the damn number!"

Dudas huffed and reluctantly dialed the number from a small, Chase Anderson business card. He handed me the phone and sat back; arms folded. Five rings before a woman answered.

"Good morning, Miami Police."

"Can I speak to Peterson?" I asked.

"He's not in the office at this time. Can I leave a message?"

"Is there another number where I can reach him?"

"Ask for someone else," Dudas said through a sigh.

"Who is calling, please?"

"A friend of Officer Anderson."

"Hold please," she said before classical music played through the phone.

"What did she say to that?" Dudas asked and picked the kitchen chairs off the floor.

"She put me on hold—"

"Peterson here," the voice was deep and somewhat horse.

"Peterson. This is . . . I know what happened to Chase Anderson."

"Identify yourself or I'm hanging up."

"Butch Sands," I said and watched Dudas nearly lose his mind.

"What happened last night?" Peterson asked all business.

"Chase is dead."

The line went silent for several seconds. Dudas leaned over in an act of frustration. He tossed paperwork in the trash and set broken coffee mug pieces along the kitchen countertop.

"Hello—"

"Anderson told me about your probable capture. I know where he said you were. But where are you now?" Peterson asked in a lower voice.

"I escaped. Chase helped me do it . . . He saved my life."

"Are you still in Florida?" Peterson whispered.

"Yes," I said and shrugged my shoulders at Dudas.

"What's he asking you, Sands?" Dudas asked and paced through the office.

"Chief Diggs is meeting with Tatum Jones today," Peterson said. "He probably tried to visit your editor last night."

"Yeah, they trashed our office."

"They both want Anderson dead," Peterson's voice went even lower. "They'll kill you and your brother unless you leave town . . . now."

"Can you help us?"

"Get out of town. Stay quiet for a few months before telling your story."

"Don't you want the story? I have enough now."

"They already want you dead. Next will be your fiancée, Hailey. Then her family . . . friends."

"How do you know—"

"If you want to live, leave Pedro Island and don't come back." Peterson sounded distracted with something. He covered the phone before it went silent.

I listened to the dial tone. Peterson was not what I had expected. He spoke in a scripted way and sounded uninterested that Chase was dead. Maybe he knows more than he lets on.

"What the hell happened?"

"I don't know." I headed for the front door. "I'll be back."

"You can't leave, Sands. We have a story to write," Dudas said and followed me through the office. "What did he say?"

"What good is that to you? You're not the one running for your life. You don't have a brother to save."

"You're damn right about that. My ass would be halfway to Mexico by now. I'd have boarded a plane hours ago."

"I need to talk to Kevin, alone," I said and walked out.

The morning sun peaked out from behind scattered rain clouds and brightened Tarpon Marina as I jogged along the golf cart trail that paralleled Palm Avenue. Long white sailboats filled every available berth. I hurried by the marina office and stopped in front of the boat from last night. I waited for Kevin and walked along the far dock just as a school of mullet circled a flats boat. Two brown pelicans stood on a wooden piling nearby. Kevin appeared and walked toward me along the opposite seawall.

"Dudas didn't leave a key," Kevin said, smoking a cigarette. "We'll have to check the boat."

"Was anyone in the marina office?" I asked and noticed a seaplane overhead. "Expecting anyone else?"

"No," Kevin said and looked up with bloodshot eyes. "You ever call Miami PD?"

"I actually talked to Peterson an hour ago."

"Peterson? What did he say?"

"Diggs will be here, today. And Tatum might still be alive. That's what it sounded like anyway. Peterson didn't want to tell me anything."

"Did you tell Peterson about Chase?"

"Yeah, but it didn't bother him for some reason. Almost like he knew something I didn't."

The seaplane descended as it passed over the marina before disappearing behind a row of tall pine trees. I watched it wondering who was on board.

"That could be anyone up there," Kevin said and brushed by me. "We still have to go out there."

"We need keys first."

Kevin stepped down on the deck and searched under chairs, through compartments full of paperwork and unused flares. There was no extra key to be found. He kicked one of the live wells shut and stepped back up on the dock.

"I told him more than once," Kevin said and started walking back toward the marina.

"Dudas should be in the news building," I said and followed.

"Let's take one of the golf carts back."

"Hold on for a second," I said and waited for Kevin to stop.

"Let's talk on the way over," Kevin said and pointed out a table near the side of the dry storage.

"I want to talk to you about Chase, first," I said and sat down on one of the patio chairs. "Sit down for a minute."

Kevin asked and tossed a pack of cigarettes on the table and sat down. "What about him? He's dead."

"Chase swore that Peterson was his guy. I think he's in narcotics. Chase said he would help us if anything happened."

"Then we should call him back before anything else happens," Kevin said and lit a cigarette.

"He said he trusted Peterson."

"Yeah, but did you ever trust Chase?"

"He told me some disturbing things out there," I said and pulled a cigarette out of the pack and lit it. "I trust him now."

"You think he's still alive?"

"There's no way he survived that," I said and inhaled the smoke without coughing. "Tatum shot him."

"Did you see it?"

"No . . . I heard it."

"What else did Chase say?"

"He started to say something about the lighthouse."

"Damn. Dudas didn't tell you?"

"Tell me what?"

"A seaplane crashed in front of it four days ago. They found two dead Cubans and ten kilos of cocaine after the fire was finally put out. Everything scattered across the beach. The lighthouse is ruined."

"Who crashed into it? Why didn't you mention that last night? Or today?"

"I was just thinking about you and your health. Still look like shit, bro."

"I can't believe you wouldn't say something about something like that?"

"Supposedly they were shot down."

"When was that?"

"Same night you disappeared."

"So, the lighthouse burned down?"

"That's right."

I thought about the times I fished the pass when I was younger, and how my father would tell me stories about the lighthouse; how it was built, who it had saved from storms, and the importance of it being built on the point of the island. I asked Hailey to marry me on top of that lighthouse.

Kevin looked down at his cell phone. "Forgot about a fishing charter this afternoon. They called me almost a year ago to schedule."

"What time?"

"Fifteen minutes from now," Kevin said, no longer relaxed. "I think they were Tobacco executives from Lexington."

"Aren't you going to cancel?"

"Let me make a phone call," Kevin said and stood up and walked toward the marina office.

I noticed three men dressed in flower shirts and bright colored shorts. They stopped Kevin near the loading dock. Two of them carried a big white cooler. All three were pale and wore sunglasses. The one not holding anything waved his arms when he spoke. He looked to be pleading with Kevin.

Chapter Twenty-Five

Kevin idled the thirty-two-foot center console, *Willy's Hooker* along the current while I sat in the stern and scanned Cayo Costa Island. We were fifty or so yards away from the beach off the starboard side. The afternoon sun was unbearably hot, and the unusually empty pass made for easy access to notable fishing holes near the shelf where the depth dropped off considerably. The larger tarpon were rolling. They were tangled in splashing schools and dove deep in the current, feeding on smaller blue crab and squirrelfish.

We idled around the South end of the island and passed flooded mangroves. The early morning rain clouds had pushed east, and the usually loud seagulls and nervous pelicans were nonexistent.

"Do you think that was Tatum's seaplane?" I asked.

"I don't know," Kevin said as he watched the tide move.

A buzzing sound came from above us. I spotted another seaplane. The pilot flew in low. Kevin accelerated the outboard engines full throttle. Water splashed up on the deck.

"Those planes looked identical. You think they'd be able to see our faces from that height?"

"Maybe," Kevin said.

"That's the plane. That's Tatum," I said.

"How do you know that?"

"Look at the tail. It has Lacosta painted on it."

Kevin redirected our route away from the island. The center console turned back toward Pedro Island. I studied the ruined lighthouse for the first time. It was surreal to see the blank spaces above charred rubble. The lighthouse of my youth once stood for all that was good about

Pedro Island. Now it reminded me of everything that had gone wrong over the past few weeks.

"Where are you going?" I asked and turned to watch the seaplane touchdown in the pass. "Did Captain Dan make it home?"

"Yeah," Kevin said with his entire focus on the now floating seaplane.

"Just pull in along the beach. Maybe he's at home."

"Right. You could call Peterson, again. Make sure he knows that Tatum's here."

I watched the seaplane taxi toward Cayo Costa. The pilot ignored us completely. It was too far away to see who it was.

"They don't seem to care about us. Maybe it's not him," Kevin said and slowed the engine to turn the wheel away from a sand bar.

"Meet me at my place in an hour," I said and jumped out in waist deep water. "This is good right here."

"Be careful with the current. It's strong in places," Kevin said and killed the engine.

The sand bar was close enough for me to walk. I shuffled both feet to avoid stingrays. The current pulled at my waist until I walked up to the empty beach.

I jogged along the shoreline, feeling the pain in my leg for the first time in days. The decimated lighthouse was hard to look at with yellow caution tape surrounding the beaten structure. The roof was black with gaping holes. Two of the stilts were broken, causing the entire house to lean to one side. The giant light bulb was gone, as was the tin roof. All that remained was the iron railing once circling the top deck. It stood on end against sweltered boards and melted siding. The most astonishing sight was the tail of the seaplane, sticking out from the rubble. No wings. No cockpit.

I thought about the many hours spent in the lighthouse, sitting behind the railing and watching the pass. The times Hailey and I had watched the setting sun from up there. I remembered the time we made love beneath the shining light, and the way she moved above me. I could still see the glow in her brown eyes the night I proposed, and she said yes. These thoughts helped to mask the leg pain during the long walk to Captain Dan's house.

I finally arrived but no one was home, and the house was locked. I sat on the steps under the cover of canopy that led up to the porch and wiped my sandy feet. I thought about where Tatum would look for me first, and who might be with him. I still believed Dudas would lie to protect me, regardless of the money they would offer him. New clouds rolled in, and it started to rain again. I found an old beach bike along the side of the house and walked it across the wide road. Peddling proved much easier than walking, even with an old rusty bike. I coasted through a hard rain and was at the back door of the news building within fifteen minutes.

I wiped the water off my face and walked through the back door. Dudas sat alone at the kitchen table. The room smelled of body odor and stale coffee. He flipped the lights on.

"Chief Diggs was just here," Dudas said, staring at his coffee mug.

"Was he alone?"

"Yes."

"What did you say to him?"

"That you had been gone for days. And that I had no idea when you were coming back."

"Where did I go?"

"Mexico to visit Hailey," Dudas said with a sigh. "A place you should actually be."

"We've been over that."

"What about the story? Can we at least make this hiding business worth something?" Dudas said and patted a blank pad of paper next to him on the table. "Where did you go this morning?"

"With Kevin to—"

"What for? Isn't there enough going wrong?"

"Tatum landed his plane in the pass, right in front of us."

"Did he see you?" Dudas said and rolled his eyes. "I don't know."

"What do you know?"

"Can I trust you?" I felt strange asking.

"What do you think? I've known your family for years. Why would I lie to you now?" Dudas asked and picked up a pencil and looked at me.

"You want to do this *now*?"

"When would you suggest? Diggs said he was getting coffee and would be back within the hour." Dudas said and pointed at the kitchen clock. "That was twenty minutes ago."

"I'm going to one of Chase Anderson's inside guys with this story. I don't trust Diggs or anyone else."

"I know. But you really should think about telling me what you know and then buying the next plane ticket to Mexico. You need to get the hell out of here for a month. I can turn what you tell me into a story. Just give me your notes and what you know. I'll even explain everything to Kevin."

"This story is bigger than this newspaper. You can clear your name, too," Dudas said and scribbled something down.

I pulled my wallet out and opened it. A stack of folded papers fell out from where money should be. I quickly sorted through the stack and unfolded each piece.

"Most of it's here. The rest I can remember. These notes help me remember. Like pieces to a puzzle," I said and slid the stack across the table to Dudas.

"What about Peterson? Have you called Peterson yet?" Dudas asked as he read some of the notes.

"No. I think Diggs was acting as Peterson on the phone this morning. I'm going to call him again."

"I'll work with this, but you really do need to leave. We can discuss further over the phone."

"Leave now?" I asked and stepped back from the table.

"Yes, leave Pedro Island right now. They want you dead. Game's over."

I thought about Kevin and his situation. There was no scenario where he could finish things with Tatum Jones alone. We started this together and would end it together.

"I'm not leaving Kevin. He needs me."

"Staying is a death wish. Rose dying is a tragedy. But it is Kevin's tragedy to deal with, not yours. You still have a life with Hailey and this newspaper."

I watched Dudas and wondered if what he said was true, or if he was speaking from another place. It was hard to trust anyone now. Even Dudas.

"Don't lose those notes," I said before hurrying outside.

"Get out of here, Sands. Call me in a week and we'll sort this story out."

Black clouds covered the island and a cool rain fell. I peddled the bike as fast as I could down a side street. Coconut palms and banyan trees moved past me in a scattered mix of greens and grays. The rain felt good on my face and arms. I turned down another side street that paralleled Palm Avenue and raced an elderly couple on a golf cart across a stretch of shell filled road.

Chapter Twenty-Six

I pulled the bike off the road and watched Kevin light a cigarette from a short distance. He leaned against the cover of a banyan tree as rain continued to fall. He nervously smoked the cigarette and checked his watch as I rolled the bike onto a spread of palm fronds.

"Sorry I'm late," I said.

"Where in the hell have you been?" Kevin asked as he turned to look at me.

I scanned the area and waited for two cars to pass in either direction before crossing. My paranoia for Tatum Jones and whoever else might appear made everything feel urgent. Even talking felt like a risk.

"Tatum's here, on Pedro Island," I said.

"I know. Dudas called me at your place," Kevin said and looked down at my injured leg. "Why the bike? Thought your leg was better."

"It stings. Forget about my leg. What did Dudas say?"

"He wants us to disappear for a month or two. Let the police sort everything out. Thinks we're dead if we don't."

"What do you want, Kevin?"

"You know what I want. But you should leave. Fly to Mexico and be with Hailey. She's your future. Mine's over."

His tone was low but strong and unwavering. We shared an unspoken understanding. There was no avoiding this. His fate was sealed as soon as Rose quit breathing. The vision of Kevin, a towering ten-year-old reeling in a hundred-pound tarpon, burned in my long-term memory. Childhood heroes are not overpaid athletes.

They are giants from our youth. Kevin was bigger than life then, and he showed me how to land a silver king through actions, not words. I could never tell him what not to do. He was a god.

"Tatum won't be alone. He'll have at least twenty of them with him. We could find help somewhere else and come back."

"I'm not running anymore." Kevin said and lit another cigarette. "We should have finished this in New Orleans. Where's the truck?"

"I left it parked at your place."

"Let's walk."

We stayed on the side road parallel to Palm Avenue until we could see the center of town. There was a covered area between an office building and art gallery. I leaned in against the side of the art gallery to keep from being seen. A taller man stood in front of the Catholic Church next to the lone gas station and three blocks away from Marker 17 Tavern. He looked out of place. His hair was long, and he was dressed in all black. He was not the usual snowbird in a bright orange cabana shirt and sandals. There was no look of displacement or excitement for seagulls and palm trees.

"Do you recognize him?" I asked.

"No way." Kevin said and leaned in beside me. "What's he holding?"

A middle-aged couple was window-shopping ten yards away. The man held an umbrella out over the woman, keeping pace with her along the sidewalk. They walked past a small group of locals looking for cover from the rain.

The man in front of the church appeared to be praying. He made the sign of the cross three times and kissed a necklace hanging down over the faded black shirt. Next, he pulled something chrome out of his pants pocket.

"Is that a gun?" Kevin asked.

"Gun?" I asked and pushed away from our cover.

"Is that Tatum?" Kevin asked and grabbed my arm, pulling me back, to keep me from being seen.

"Yes." I said and pulled away from the attempted restraint and stepped back to avoid an approaching golf cart. "Do you see anyone else?"

Tatum noticed us staring and turned away from the church. He stuffed the gun back in his pants pocket and walked toward us. I recognized the tattooed arms and light skin as he drew closer. He wore the same flip-flops, but without the double-breasted suit. His long black shorts and faded black shirt made him stick out in front of the stucco-white church.

"Turn around without making it obvious," Kevin said with his back against the wall. "Is he looking—"

"Sands," Tatum said and slowed his pace.

"Butch," Kevin said in a whisper.

"Get the truck," I said and waved for Kevin to be silent. "He doesn't see you."

"Stay out in the open. He won't do anything in public."

"The truck."

"Dammit," Kevin said and ran off.

"We need to talk," I said and walked out to meet Tatum.

"What's there to talk about?"

"There are witnesses everywhere," I said and pointed at a man pumping gasoline at the station across the street.

"You're right," Tatum said and smiled as he waved at two girls on a golf cart. "Such a busy time of year."

"Is Chase dead?"

"Probably," Tatum said and pointed the gun at me. "Look familiar?"

The nervous feeling that came with having a gun pointed at me returned and my stomach sank. I welcomed the scenario as a step in the right direction, a step to end the madness. There was no dark room or locked door.

"What about Diggs?" I asked and watched the barrel of his .357 Desert Eagle.

"On re-assignment in Key West," he said and stepped within a few feet of me. "He's meeting with your brother, probably as we speak."

"Fine. What next?"

"Coffee," he said and motioned toward Marker 17 Tavern. "Espresso maybe?"

I followed him across the median toward Marker 17 Tavern. A blue heron flew over us and landed on the roof of the church. My eyes were drawn to the red tile roof and palm trees surrounding the church. I watched the lanky bird watching me. Every detail of the street and the church and the road and the front door of Marker 17 came to life. It was as if this was the last time, I would ever see the outside world. The screen door opened, and Tatum waited for me to walk inside toward an inevitable fate.

Tatum sat down near the front window and placed the hand cannon on a round table. I sat across from him as Joe approached us. He noticed the gun and froze. There were only a few locals eating in the back dining area. They were clueless of the situation.

"I need a couple of menus, Joe," I said.

"How's the coffee here?" Tatum asked in a serious tone.

"All right, I guess," Joe said.

"Good," Tatum said and scanned the bar. "Cream and sugar?"

"Sure."

"Are you hungry?" I asked and reached around the gun to move a used ashtray off the table.

"Just coffee," Tatum said and looked out the window.

"I'll be right back," Joe said and walked toward the bar.

"Enough bullshit, Butch. Tell me what Chase Anderson told you about my operation?" Tatum asked and put his palm on the gun. "And then tell me how one of my seaplanes just crashes into a lighthouse."

"I was locked in a cage when it happened."

Joe came back and placed two menus on the table. He acted nervous as Tatum read from the back page.

"Do you serve fair trade coffee?" Tatum asked, watching Joe watch the loaded gun.

"Let me check on that," Joe said and turned to walk toward the kitchen.

Tatum looked frustrated. He pushed the menu to one side of the table just as someone caught his attention outside. He watched them walk past the window.

I leaned forward. "Chase told me everything he knows about you."

"You mean, *knew* about me. Be careful with your word choice."

Joe hurried back to our table and stood over us shaking his head at Tatum.

"That's fine," Tatum said. "Bring two cups anyway."

"Be right back," Joe said and turned away.

Tatum watched an older woman enter the bar. She wore a white sundress and leather sandals. Her hair was bleach-blonde, and her breasts were augmented. She carried a small white poodle.

"What's everything, Butch? And does your oversized editor know what you know . . . yet?" Tatum asked and looked at the woman. "You're only alive because I haven't killed you."

"I never asked for any of this."

"Why not leave it alone then? You could have left it alone after the gas station. But you followed me."

"You almost killed me."

"But I didn't. Be glad for that."

Chasing Palms

Joe set a two steaming cups of black coffee between us along with a bowl of creamer. His hands were shaking, and he would not look either one of us in the eyes.

"Thanks, Joe," I said.

"Anytime," Joe said and walked away.

"Gracias," Tatum said. He put the steaming cup to his nose and smelled the aroma before taking a drink. "Good." He set the cup down.

I poured in cream and sugar. "How did you get involved with Chief Diggs?"

"He came to me first, but I will tell you something. A police chief is good for business. A journalist can only be costly."

"Then why are you here now?"

"To fix a few problems. Chase was my first problem, but that's over now. He's back in Miami now, working the strip on a bike."

"Wait, Chase is alive?"

"Of course, he's alive. See, a detective is even more valuable than a chief."

I pushed my coffee away and stood up. Tatum motioned for me to sit back down. Another group of locals walked in. The bar was getting crowded.

"We're going out to Cayo Costa this evening. I'm not giving you a choice."

"Tonight?"

"Diggs has coordinated a sting. You'll be there to take the fall for fifty kilos of cocaine. Ten to fifteen years max if you make parole. Dudas knows to write a story about a shady journalist gone rouge. This way, everything resets, and all eyes are off my operation."

"And if I don't?"

"I'll kill you and Hailey."

"I need a minute in the bathroom."

"No chance. I don't trust you."

"I'll be right back."

Despite Tatum's order, I stood up and wandered across the room, down the hallway toward the place I slept in last night. I knew the crowded bar was my best defense.

"Butch," Joe said from the kitchen. "In here."

Joe whispered, "Chief Diggs is here."

"Where?"

"Kitchen."

"Is he alone?"

Joe nodded yes then walked out toward the bar to serve a daiquiri to a woman in a white sundress. He changed out a fifty-dollar bill and waited for the woman to walk back to her table.

"What did he say?" I asked and pointed at the special's menu on the wall behind the bar.

"He went through your room first. Now, he's waiting for you to come back."

"What's he doing?"

"Eating lobster," Joe said and turned his back on me and began washing beer mugs. "Turn around, Butch."

Tatum approached me at the bar. He carried the cup of coffee in one hand and held the gun down to his side in the other.

"What are you two talking about?" Tatum asked.

"I was thanking him for letting me sleep here last night," I said. "Let's go back to—"

"You slept here last night," Tatum said as he sipped his coffee. "Bullshit."

"Why would I lie about that?"

"Come outside," Tatum said and set his coffee on the bar.

Chasing Palms

I followed him outside to the street. Rain fell at a steady pace. Palm Avenue was quiet and vacant of any locals.

"Did you see him?" Tatum asked and held up his gun.

"See who?"

"Chief Diggs was watching us from the kitchen. I noticed him when we first sat down at the table," Tatum said as he pulled a clip from the magazine and re-loaded his gun. "We need to get out of the street."

I knew the news building and Kevin's house were both obvious places for Chief Diggs to look. A moment of uncertainty followed. Tatum looked down the street.

"The church," Tatum said and gave me a slight push. "You go inside first."

We jogged across the empty street. My leg was hurting, but the pain was less than before. It was the thought of being shot at again that kept me moving until we reached the front entrance of the church. I opened the door and scrambled inside. Tatum followed me in and closed the door behind us.

The church was dark and smelled of wood varnish and wax. A dim light pushed in through the red and blue stain-glass windows. Rain pelted the roof and a steady thunder faded above.

"Why didn't you say something?" I asked.

"Hello!" Tatum's voice echoes through the vacant chapel.

There was no answer. I found an empty pew and sat down. Tatum stood by the cracked door, peeking out.

"Why were you here earlier?" I asked.

"It's obvious," Tatum said and closed the door. "Why do people go to church?"

"Forget it. Dudas is editing the story I gave before you kidnapped me. I have nothing else to do with the final print."

"I know. He told me that." Tatum's gun made a hollow sound when he dropped it on a pew.

"Then what are we doing?"

"You may not have pulled the trigger. But you're still one of two reasons June Bug is dead. I cannot forgive you for that. So, I need you to do one favor. After this is done, we're done. You can tell anybody who'll listen how loco I am. I could care less. Who's going to stop me anyway?"

"But what can—"

"Listen," Tatum said and lit a match.

I turned around in the pew. Tatum's narrow face glowed with the flame. The marijuana smoke came next. He filled his lungs and exhaled.

"My family is the only important thing for me. The money is easy. Women are even easier. But when my family dies, you and your brother die. Chase will eventually get his. That's a promise."

The words were amplified in the church. I was sorry about June Bug's death for the first time. He wasn't just another drug dealer. He was someone's brother.

"Is your brother coming after you? I saw him leave earlier. But the keys were still in the truck this afternoon," Tatum said and went back to the door and opened it. "I want him to suffer for pulling the trigger. I want him to know that his actions ultimately caused all of this." More coughing followed. "We'll go out to the island tonight and Chief Diggs will arrest you and maybe your brother, too."

"I don't believe Diggs is in on this."

"He's in. It has to look official."

He held his watch up to the light.

"I don't know where Kevin is."

"Right."

"Why didn't you just settle this in the bar?"

"I could ask you the same question," he said and took another hit from the joint and put it out on the floor of the church.

I thought about the days before. Everything seemed so distant in my mind. I had forgotten most of it with the near drowning. None of it was clear. All I knew was that Chase was alive, and Kevin will be coming for me soon.

"When's this happening?"

"Follow me," Tatum said and ran down the aisle. He passed the podium and stopped to make the sign of the cross below a hanging crucifix of Jesus.

Chapter Twenty-Seven

Tarpon Marina was empty of the usual tourists and locals with the afternoon thunderstorm. A forklift operator moved boats into dry storage. I watched him lift a thirty-foot Sea-Ray out of the water. Tatum led me around the back of the bait and fueling docks. A seaplane had been winched halfway up the dry hanger. I recognized the seaplane from when it landed in the pass. *Lacosta* was spelled out on the tail.

The Cape Dory Explorer was next on his list. I watched her being lowered in the water. The same frantic forklift operator tilted long forks and dropped her down. I never imagined her in the water. Seeing the navy-blue haul submerged was strange.

"We'll use this mess of a boat. The engines are still good, I think," Tatum said and walked up to the seaplane. "I bought it off the harbormaster. He said it's a Cape Dory or something. Said it has fair value. Seemed perfect for what we're doing." He walked along one of the seaplane floats and stepped up inside the cockpit.

I stood admiring the boat that was too expensive to buy on an honest journalist's salary. The soft blue hull was rough in places, and the dark wood molding seemed to absorb the saltwater. The captain's chair had torn fabric in places, and the buoys were not fully inflated and infested with barnacles. I studied the full forty feet from bow to stern and wondered how she would hold up.

The diesel outboards gurgled and clanked through the harbor. Tatum kept pointing out imperfections and kicking the throttle when she would stop running. He would pull the trap doors open and step down inside the hull to adjust the throttle and bang on the sparkplugs.

Tatum deliberately shut the engine down once we reached the pass and obsessively checked the magazine of his gun for bullets. I watched a boat drifting farther out in the gulf and hoped it was Kevin, or Dudas, or anyone.

"You're dropping me on the north end of the island," Tatum said after he changed into bright green swimming trunks and a white shirt. "I need to walk the whole island," he said and slipped on water-booties.

"What do I do?"

Tatum started the engine again and steered the Cape Dory in the opposite direction from where the abandoned fishing house was on Cayo Costa Island. He stayed within twenty yards of the beach. I noticed the ebb tide current that nearly killed me the night before.

* * *

Rain fell at a steady pace now with heavy cloud cover. Tatum took off his shirt and stepped down rusted steps off the bow and eased into the moving gulf water. Tattoos covered both arms. A black cross covered his back, surrounded by different tribal symbols I had never seen. Tattoos covered most of his brown skin.

He held the gun overhead and kicked through the choppy water before standing waist deep, ten yards out from the mangroves.

"Go around this way," Tatum said and pointed in the direction we had been going. "Stay close. I won't hesitate to shoot if you run."

I wanted to turn the boat around and make a run for it, but something stopped me from going. Something told me to see the plan through, to finish the story. I was tired of running and knew Kevin would show up soon and finish it.

Tatum jogged out of the water onto the vacant beach and made an open-handed gesture before he disappeared inside a line of palm trees. I pushed the throttle forward and coasted along the shoreline and eased the Cape Dory around the South end toward where the abandoned fishing house stood and killed the engine. There was no one waiting. I tossed the anchor and pulled the line until the cleats dug down into the sandy bottom.

I kicked off my shoes and grabbed an old filleting knife from the galley below. The thought of seeing Chase alive seemed impossible. I took the keys from the ignition and secured them in one of my shorts pockets before jumping overboard. The saltwater soothed my bruised face as I swam with both arms and kicked with my good leg. I reached the shoreline and walked up to the stilts beneath the house. The Cape Dory had turned some, but the anchor line seemed to hold well.

I stood beneath the cover of the house for a few minutes to think about what might happen and finally walked up the worn steps to the first floor. I expected Chief Diggs's arrival and walked down the same hallway to the very room that imprisoned me. The same empty tin plate was turned over at the top of the steps. I walked over it and stood silent in the hallway looking out at the roof and the moving water below.

I stood in front of the room with the idea to burn the place down. Both pockets were empty and wet. No lighter or matches to be found. What a sight it would be to see this wreck of a house burn with the rain. The smoke bellowing out from the boarded-up windows would be something to see.

A vile smell came from inside the room. I could see the scattered piles of crab-traps. The corner where I once laid was empty, with the bottles of rum placed side by side against the wall. A few chairs were overturned in the center of the room, and a spear gun hung from the far wall. But there was no visible explanation for the overwhelming odor.

I continued down the hall toward the adjacent room and walked up the stairs leading to the roof. The stairs were clear, but the smell worsened with each step up. My aching leg was becoming a nuisance again.

The roof was vacant, and the smell of rain helped mask the lingering funk. I walked over to the edge where I jumped to freedom and looked down at the way the edge of the beach made a sudden twenty-foot drop off that probably saved my life.

Pedro Island looked different, with the empty space where the fallen lighthouse once stood. An island treasure was now just a pile of wood and rubble from this distance. Only the long gray beach with the backdrop of tall pines and scattered palms with the occasional beachfront property were visible. I scanned the gray waterline back along the mangrove coastline of Cayo Costa to where the long sand bar pushed out a hundred yards or so into the darker blue water. The undeveloped island had no other houses, beside the dire structure I stood atop now. There were only dense mangroves and wonderful inlets for flats fishing. The open areas were merely sand and sea oats. Seagulls and white egrets populated the green mangrove tops, with the occasional blue heron stalking fish from beneath the vegetation along the shoreline.

I sat down with both feet dangling over the edge and waited for Chief Diggs. My leg welcomed the rest, and the cool rain calmed my nerves. I closed my eyes and rested back on my hands. After minutes of silence, the sound from a gun chamber being loaded caught my full attention. I stayed facing forward and prayed that maybe something else made the sound.

"Where's Tatum Jones?" a deep voice asked.

"When'd you get here?" I asked without looking back.

"You're caught in the middle, Butch," the man said and approached to kneel to my level. "I'm not sure what you know or don't know. I should've put your ass in county jail the moment we met in Miami. Chase never was a good judge of character."

"Where's Chase?"

"No idea," the man said.

"So, he could still be alive?"

"I don't think you understand what's happening here. I told Tatum to explain it to you. Didn't he explain it?"

"I watched Tatum shoot Chase," I said and scrambled to my feet and turned to look Chief Diggs in his round black sunglasses. "I didn't have a—"

"Have a what?" Chief Diggs asked and adjusted his pressed suit. Sweat beaded off his forehead. He pulled a handkerchief and wiped the back of his neck and around his sunglasses.

"When's the last time you two talked?" I asked.

"I've been trying to track his location for weeks. Your call to Peterson at the station was the first news we'd received since Chase called from New Orleans."

"The same Peterson?" I asked and realized the answer before Diggs said anything.

"Peterson is a code name," Chief Diggs said and put the gun away. Chase used it to conceal his identity. When you called asking for Peterson, I knew something had happened. Who did that to your face?"

"Tatum Jones. Wait, there's no Peterson. Bullshit, there has to be a Peterson. Why wouldn't Chase tell me Peterson was a cover?"

"Because he's a liar. I have a warrant for his arrest, too."

"But he's your—"

"Found a few hundred kilos from the county vault stashed in his apartment last week. Matter of fact, we found it the very same morning you showed up at the station."

"You're a liar."

"Tatum Jones is Anderson's *real* partner. But that only scratches the surface with him. We'll have plenty to talk about when this is over. You need to cooperate and do exactly what I tell you to do. No arguing. Cooperation will only lessen a possible sentence for trafficking to go along with the long list of other violations currently sitting on my desk in Miami."

"I'm a journalist, not a drug dealer," I said, still not believing him. "I'm innocent."

Diggs pulled a walkie-talkie from his pocket. He pressed the side button and turned away from our conversation. I scanned the area for Tatum Jones.

"Go for Sampson," Chief Diggs said.

"Go for Chief Diggs. We're along the perimeter, sir. It's clear," Sampson said in a deep voice.

"Remember, on my mark."

"Yes, sir."

Chief Diggs looked past me. A sputtering outboard engine came from behind him. I turned and saw a flats boat. The man driving wore a red baseball hat and dark sunglasses that concealed his face. He fired a gunshot overhead and ran the boat ashore. Broad shoulders turned toward us, and he was slow to move out of his seat. The boat was on shore now and he tied the mooring line around the narrow trunk of a coconut palm.

"Don't make any sudden moves," Diggs said. "Just stand there and wait for him."

I recognized Tatum Jones standing on the far end of the beach, fifty yards away. The other man hurried up the steps toward the first floor. Their momentum slowed on the floor below. Then nothing came. No hurried footsteps toward the roof. All sound stopped. Chief Diggs moved to the side of the stairway with gun drawn. His eyes were planted on me while he waited for either of them to appear.

A chainsaw started below us. Chief Diggs made a calming gesture at me and covered his nose and mouth before starting down the steps.

The chainsaw ripped through rotten wood at a fast pace. A vibration shot across the roof. The awful smell had worsened.

I wondered what they were doing in the room below and had no idea what they were cutting out from behind the walls. Chief Diggs eased his way down the steps. Once he was gone there was only the buzzing saw. Tatum was no longer on the beach, so I knew he had to be close.

Two gunshots fired, followed by a scream. The buzzing continued with the vibration from the walls. I scrambled over to the steps and waited for Chief Diggs to reappear. No one came. For several seconds, I pondered the next move. My leg still bothered me, but it hurt less given an adrenaline rush. I finally decided to run. No way was I jumping again.

Down the steps, the buzzing sound was deafening. I stepped over a dead body and ran past both rooms. Another gunshot came from inside the second room, and I opened the door. Kevin had lost the red hat and glasses in the struggle and stood looking down two-gun barrels at Tatum Jones. Blood ran down Tatum's cheek, but he showed no sign of pain or fear. Kevin held aim like a statue. He glanced at me for a second and a smile lifted his bearded chin.

"Here we are," Kevin said. "You want to run, don't you?"

Tatum fell to one knee and glanced down at the filthy floor. His head shook in frustration. Tension filled the room.

"Go on, run like you always do," Kevin said. "Cowards run . . . are you a coward, Tone?"

Tatum looked over at me and shrugged. The moment made me forget about Chief Diggs. This was a lifetime in the making, and more than a week of chaos. This moment was everything for Kevin. Dead or alive, Tatum Jones made no difference to either of us. Dead or alive,

Kevin would always be a lost soul with a warrant. He would be running from this for the rest of his life.

"Don't do it," I said. "Chief Diggs called in backup. Let the police put him on death row."

"Diggs is dead," Tatum said. "He's two rooms over, face down on a pile of crab-traps."

"Never works out that way, Butch," Kevin said still holding his mark. "Rose deserves this. Lawyers will cut his sentence down to ten years with good behavior."

"Maybe five years," Tatum said smiling. "Your girlfriend doesn't concern me anyway. I've killed far more people than her. She doesn't affect my bottom line."

Voices came from the floor above us. Footsteps followed. Backup had arrived. It would not take long for them to find Chief Diggs's body. They would arrest all three of us for murder.

"Come on Kev," I said. "Let's get out of here now. Forget about Tatum—"

"Go ahead, Butch," Kevin said. "I'll be right out. Just give me a second alone with him."

I looked at Kevin and knew his mind was made up. There was nothing I could do to stop him. He was not the same person, and this was not a good situation. Tatum Jones was a dead man.

"Meet me on the beach," I said. "I understand."

I ran out and hurried down the other steps but missed one and fell hard into the wet sand. I rolled into a patch of sea oats for cover and listened to the voices up top. A long silence followed before multiple gunshots caused panic and everyone on the top floor took cover.

Kevin appeared and ran from the room with both guns in hand. He jumped down the steps and pulled me to my feet then pushed me inside the cover of mangroves. His eyes were wildly keen and blue and focused.

"Not a sound," Kevin said.

Three men wearing black SWAT gear and toting heavy firearms hustled toward the steps leading up to the first floor. One of the men held a walkie-talkie to his ear before throwing it down in the sand. The three of them raced up the steps.

"It's over now," Kevin said. "Made him look me in the eyes and pulled both triggers. Tone is dead."

A bevy of gunshots sounded off. One of the police officers ran down the steps but was shot in the back before he could reach the sand. He landed face first on the beach. Kevin pushed me away from the house toward the interior of the island. Another round of gunshots came shortly after.

"Follow me," Kevin said and used his hands to shield the mangrove leaves and thin branches. "Place will turn into a blood bath once Tatum's guys show up and find him."

"Diggs told me the truth about Chase. Why didn't you say something in New Orleans?" I asked.

"Why would I say anything you didn't need to know? So, what if Chase Anderson is a dirty cop. He did what he had to do. No shame in that."

"I thought you hated him."

"I do. But he found me at Tarpon Marina a few hours ago."

"Chase is alive?"

"He was shot once in the shoulder and once in the thigh," Kevin said trying to keep up with me. "I made him go to the hospital. He had lost too much blood and would have probably died. He desperately wanted to be out here to finish what we started."

We ran through sugar sand toward the Cape Dory and pushed her off the beach. I stepped up a side rail and turned the ignition key. Kevin followed up the same rail and fell into the bow. Gunshots came from up the beach. We had been spotted.

"Go, Butch," Kevin said and fired shots back toward the abandoned house. "I'll get the anchor line."

The big diesel engines fired, and I dropped the throttle back and turned her away from the beach. We were pointed east, and the bow rose as I pushed the throttle forward. She finally planed off.

Chapter Twenty-Eight

The afternoon thunderstorm continued to drench Pedro Island and the surrounding coast. I sat in the stern of the Cape Dory and felt the rain soak my aching body. Kevin sat in the Captain's Chair with low shoulders and a blank stare.

"We need to leave," I said.

"I'll get us out of here," Kevin said. "But you have nothing to worry about. They're coming for me. Not you." Kevin calmly lit a cigarette and sat back in the chair. He was calm for the first time since the evening before our trip with Rose to Miami.

"What are you thinking, Kevin?"

"You know the inlets. Take her down Gasparilla Sound and dump her."

I could never abandon the Cape Dory. She was abandoned once before. Now was the perfect opportunity to claim her as my own.

"No chance."

"This boat's a liability. Needs more work than she's worth."

I throttled forward around the North end of Pedro Island and watched Kevin sitting in the stern and realized prison was meant for some but was not an option for others. He did what most were afraid to do and put someone else's life ahead of his own. I thought about our lives together and remembered a time when he was larger than everyone and everything. A time when he slayed giant silver kings and hauled in hammer head sharks.

Our lives had grown apart since college and there was never enough time for each other. There was never a moment to sit down, fish, and truly listen to one another about what was important in our lives. Everything and everyone else always took that time without consideration.

Chasing Palms

When you are young, the time is yours and everything else can wait. The Gulf is yours, and the flats boat is your vessel in the giant pass where sharks prowl thirty feet below. The sunset is yours and no one is asking you to leave it behind. It is yours to watch and feel and wonder about until the moon pulls the tides that fill your fantasy with monsters waiting to be tamed by a twelve-year-old giant and his younger brother standing by, watching, learning, and collecting images for a story, years later, when time is out of reach.

* * *

The setting sun drew shadows across the water as I dropped Kevin off along the beach near Captain Dan's house and pushed the Cape Dory full throttle down the coast for over an hour before the gas tank went dry along the North end of Gasparilla Sound. I calmly stepped overboard, eased down into the cool saltwater and swam toward a row of white stucco houses. It was painful to leave the Cape Dory abandoned but I knew it was necessary. She slowly drifted out toward the mouth of the pass.

I finally reached a fishing dock and climbed up a ladder, dripping wet. A family sat together, around a kitchen table, eating dinner in a nearby house. The possibility of ever sharing a stress-free meal with family again seemed out of reach.

I ran through the cool damp grass between two houses and stopped where the cul-de-sac circled around just off a main road and found a gas station less than a mile away.

A group of older women gave me a snobbish look as I walked under the light of the fuel pumps. I ignored their snickers, knowing my bruised face and filthy clothes were grubby.

A middle-aged man walked out of the gas station carrying a gallon of milk and a bottle of aspirin. I took the money roll out from my wet pocket and approached his blue minivan.

"I need your help," I said and tried not to sound desperate.

"This is all I have left," he said and graciously handed over a dollar and some change before opening the driver side door.

"I don't need money," I said and showed him the stack of hundred-dollar bills. "I need you to help me with something."

"Are you in some kind of trouble, son? You look hurt."

"I need a ride somewhere. I'll pay you five hundred dollars."

"Why can't you take a cab?"

"Either you will, or you won't."

I noticed a police cruiser driving by and turned my head away from the street. Any public transportation was a risk.

"You're married, right? Take it."

"Did you rob somebody or something?"

"I can't say anything. Can you help me?"

"Where do you need to go?" he asked and sat down in the driver's seat and closed the door.

"Place is about thirty minutes South of here."

"Get in," he said and started the engine.

* * *

The man dropped me at the end of a sand filled road and I walked along the seawall toward the abandoned house on the point. An older *Indian* motorcycle leaned against the narrow wooden legs of the house. I looked up at the faded blue paint that outlined the untreated wood panels below the hurricane damaged metal roof and line of mature coconut palms. I spotted Chase Anderson in the open window on the far side of the house and hurried around the plot of sand and gravel where the concrete driveway was supposed to have been poured. Pedro Island was a distant barrier against the fast-moving water beyond the balcony. I walked up the steps and looked out at my home island without the lighthouse.

"Chase," I said and walked through the open foyer toward the backroom.

"How did you know I was here?" Chase asked. "Where's Kevin?"

"He's hiding out for a few days."

Chase smiled through the discomfort and shrugged. He was bleeding through his torn shirt and filthy shorts. Blood stained his clothes at the thigh and shoulder. He held his balance against vertical timber where drywall would never be hung.

"So, he did it then? He finished it for me."

"Yeah, Kevin did it."

He pushed away from the wall and walked across the room toward the oversized squares where pane glass windows would never be hung. He picked up a baseball off the floor and held it the way he would a two-seam fastball. The pale-yellow sun fell beyond Pedro Island in the distant waterline.

"You're not going to a hospital, are you?"

"Grace is still gone, you know," Chase said and dropped his head. "I never believed I'd see her again until now. Maybe . . . I don't know, Butch, maybe she knows and is waiting for me. I want to *believe* more than anything."

I watched him struggle to stand and questioned my reality. His soul mate had been murdered and there was nothing he could ever do about it. She was never coming back.

"If we can't be together, maybe I can die in our house," Chase said in a low whisper. "I can feel her spirit here. The pain eases some, knowing she's watching me now. If it's real, and there's a chance to be with her . . . where else could it be better for this to happen?"

Chapter Twenty-Nine

Evening set in and a steady breeze moved down Palm Avenue. The warmth of the day began to fade beyond the tall pine trees that speckled the far-off shoreline of Cayo Costa Island. I thought about Chase Anderson and the moment he died, eyes focused on the setting sun, in the middle of his abandoned house, without making a sound from the discomfort and pain. He was truly at peace.

Kevin had not spoken since I told him about Chase, not a word about police or even the snook he caught earlier this morning. He stood alone now, in the shadow of a lone palm.

I watched him from inside the *Island Courier* office. For the first time, my larger-than-life brother looked desperate and weak. His mourning for Rose grew like a mangled tree inside him. He had become a short-lived killer, deflated in size, and a small piece of a once strong shell.

I held my plane ticket for Cancun and watched a blank computer screen. My excitement for being with Hailey soon helped ease the stress of trying to write a story, proclaiming my brother's innocence. I finally decided to walk outside and hurried down the sun-bleached steps toward Kevin. I wanted to help his pain with words of encouragement but knew it would not work. Not with Kevin. Not with a heart that big.

"Kev?"

He turned to face me, eyes wide and peering. His breathing steady but unsettled. Both hands clenched, ready for a fight.

"What do you need?" I asked. "Dudas contacted Miami PD. They'll need your testimony tomorrow. You need to talk. There are no outs this time."

"I won't be here," Kevin said.

I expected this response. Kevin was a fighter who needed a fight. But the fight of his life was over and there was no possible rematch. Rose was dead and Kevin was headed for prison.

"Where will you be? You need to face this head-on. Running only proves your guilt."

Kevin smiled at the plea and stared down at the dark Bermuda grass. His head shook slightly, and he cleared his throat. For the first time in our lives, the silence between us was truly uncomfortable.

"Thank you for choosing me when Rose died. I know that was hard with your life," Kevin said still looking down. "You could've died too. Hailey might have lost you."

He lifted his head to show the gruff and trusting face that had chased a killer across Florida. He was crying. The scene was suffocating.

"Either I disappear, or we both die on this island, the same way James died."

I needed our father here, now. I wanted the whole family again. My parents and brother again, drifting for tarpon in the pass. Carefree with two lines in the water, green on the tip, on a Sunday in early April. I wanted my father's grin to ease both our minds, my mother's loving eyes telling us that everything will be okay, and my unconquerable twelve-year-old brother.

These moments were lost, and this present life swallowed the bones and marrow of childhood innocence. Kevin and I were at a crossroads in the early evening of a weather perfect day on the island that shaped both of us. Our mother was alone on a cold scenic hill overlooking the Queen City in the heart of America, clueless about her two boys and their current place in the world. She would die if she knew. It was better for her not to know.

"Where will you go?" I asked.

Kevin began to walk away at a slow pace, eyes fixated on the dark road that turned through the heart of Pedro Island. He stopped and was still for a time. The screen door of Marker 17 Tavern swung open, and the light inside caught his attention.

"Kevin . . . nobody will miss Tatum Jones."

He turned to face me. The light from the open door showed his sharp features and glossed over eyes. He cleared his throat and looked up at the evening sky. There was no moon.

"You ever feel like there isn't an answer for death or any of this?"

"With religion—"

"Forget about God. I'm talking about love and fear. Do you ever think about Hailey and your future together? Everything can be good and under control. Then one day, she does something she's done a hundred times before. Does something innocent without the first thought of fear. Ever wonder how to protect everything good in your life? Because . . . you can have the money, you can love someone more than yourself, the miracle of children and health, but you only have them for a time, and the time is pure and real and lasting until it's gone, or until something happens to you or her or them. Doesn't that scare the hell out of you? It's amazing we can be here one minute and be the victim of a stray bullet the next."

I held back tears. Life and everything sacred came to the forefront of my mind. Kevin's life had fallen apart.

"Rose was all those things for me. And I took a chance loving her. And I waited to tell her. And she's dead now. And I don't know where she went or if I'll ever see her again."

Kevin reached in his back pocket and pulled out a gun. The dark silhouette forced a reaction. I lunged forward at him, but common sense stopped me when the gun pointed directly at his temple.

"I love you, Butch. And I know the last week caused you pain . . . but that sacrifice means more to me than anything you could've ever done. I want you to enjoy your life with Hailey and everything that comes with it. You have your life. There's no need to run anymore . . . you won't ever see me again."

Kevin lowered the gun and turned away. He walked with sulking shoulders. The dark street finally covered him and there were only the offbeat sounds of shoes touching sand. His jog turned into a sprint below a row of palm trees. The sound finally faded, and a long silence followed him.

About the Author

Jonathan Herbert is a freelance writer and novelist. Born in Cincinnati, Ohio and raised in Englewood, Florida. He has been the recipient of many literary awards, including honors in the *William Faulkner Literary Competition, Great Midwest Book Festival,* and *Paris Book Festival*. After receiving a Bachelor of Arts from the University of Cincinnati, he studied literature and film in Los Angeles. He then created a Florida fiction series based on an impassioned young journalist, Butch Sands, and his unpredictable life on Pedro Island. Herbert currently lives in Cincinnati with his wife, Angela and their children, Hannah and Luke.

Upcoming New Release!

JONATHAN HERBERT'S
BUTCH SANDS SERIES
BOOK 4

LEEWARD RUN

A brilliant ex-con races against time, and a terminal diagnosis to find his estranged daughter in the chaos of Los Angeles. Daring bank heists draw journalist Butch Sands into a gripping chase across America, exploring themes of family, purpose, and the impact of choices. As alliances form and tragic events unfold, the narrative builds towards a scorching final showdown on the streets, leaving an indelible mark on characters and readers alike.

**For more information
visit: www.SpeakingVolumes.us**

Now Available!

JONATHAN HERBERT'S

Butch Sands Series
Books 1 – 2

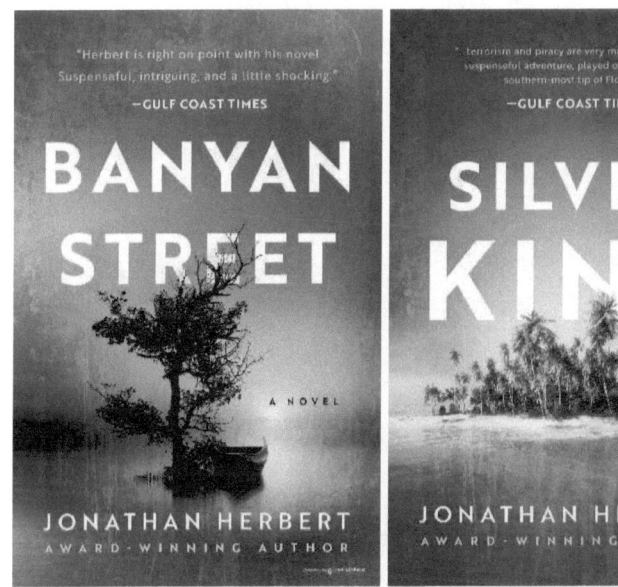

**For more information
visit:** www.SpeakingVolumes.us

Now Available!

RAY DAN PARKER'S

The Tom Williams Saga
Books 1 – 3

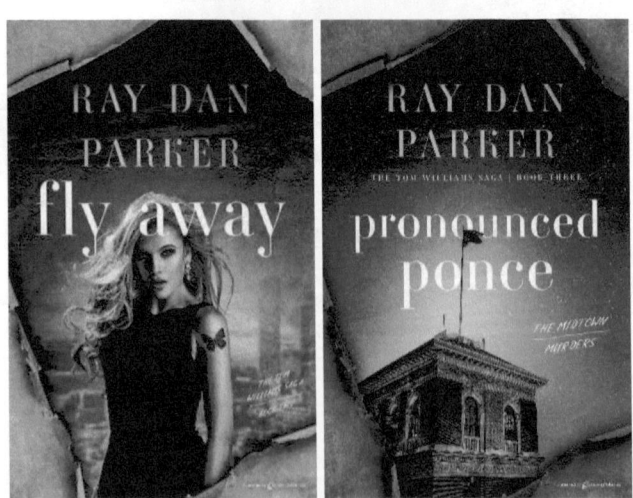

For more information visit: https://svpubs.com/3SMyAO2

Now Available!

MATTHEW J. FLYNN'S
SUSPENSE / THRILLERS

**For more information
visit:** www.SpeakingVolumes.us

Now Available!

BRIAN FELGOISE AND DAVID TABATSKY

FILTHY RICH LAWYERS SERIES
Book One – Book Two

**For more information
visit:** www.SpeakingVolumes.us

www.ingramcontent.com/pod-product-compliance
Lightning Source LLC
LaVergne TN
LVHW041659070526
838199LV00045B/1117